Life at the Market

By

Wendy Allen

Edited by Anika Klix

JOY HOUSE PUBLISHING
Kent, WA

Back cover author photo by Christina Lorraine

JOY HOUSE PUBLISHING
Kent, WA

ISBN-13: 978-1718832053

DEDICATION

This book is dedicated to my Mom and Dad, my two sons, Jessie and Mylo, my grandchildren, Oliver, Henry, Emmett, and Elsie, and to my Higher Power.

My deepest gratitude to you all.

Contents

ACKNOWLEDGMENT

Special thanks to my friend and editor, Anika Klix.

I offer my deepest gratitude for making this dream a reality.

The Family Market

"Good morning! How are you today? Paper or plastic?" Sam asked in his everyday I'm-a-Robot, I'm-a-mockingbird, I'm-a-trained-monkey, yes-I've said this five-million times, tone of voice.

The customer, a 25 year old I'm-in-a-hurry girl said, "Paper, please. I hate plastic!" She went back to looking at her iPhone.

Sam thought, *well good to know, I won't ever ask again, I will memorize your face like the back of my hand, and if you ever come through my check-out counter again, without delay I will grab that 'paper' bag!* His mind's eye rolled to the back of his head.

You see, checkers ask this question benevolent to many because paper bags cost more than plastic bags, so they really don't want to give out paper. Plastic, on the other hand, rips and ends up in the landfills waiting for the Earth to end. You can recycle paper and use it over and over again, then burn it. Unlike plastic, it just doesn't decompose. So, grocery store companies do not really want to give out paper bags. Seems trivial, doesn't it?

Essentially, it's about cost. Of course part of it is about the choice, but really, grocery stores want to give you plastic. Checkers get no real thrill asking the same darn question over and over! Thank goodness people are coming to their senses and using cloth bags now. Some cities have even banned plastic and charge extra if you don't bring your own bag; a conscientious choice.

Sam was having a good day. He rolled out of bed at 5:00 a.m., threw on his black pants, white shirt, a spritz of his favorite Calvin Klein cologne, grabbed his apron and headed out the door to open the store by 6:00 a.m. He used to keep his apron at the store where he worked, but they always went missing for some reason. He couldn't understand why because it had his name embroidered right on the front of the dang thing! Anyone who took it would be walking around with "SAM" plastered across their chest. He had never seen any of his co-workers with his apron on and couldn't fathom why anyone else would take it or would even want it.

As Sam was ringing up a large-chested, blonde bombshell who looked to be around 20 years old, wearing a very, VERY tight t-shirt that said "I ROCK!" on it and some of the lowest cut spray-on-denim shorts he had ever seen, he noticed she was buying baby oil, bubble bath, strawberries, and chocolate syrup. He thought *can I please come home with you?* Suddenly, he jolted back to reality and his thoughts drifted back to wondering if someone could have taken his apron, somehow peel his name off of it and embroider their own name on it. The thought started to really piss him off! He was on his third apron in two months. The store gave out the first one, but after that, if you lost it you had to buy another one for $5.00. It was required to wear your name tag on your apron while in the store and on shift. Sure, you could remove it when you went to use the restroom, but you had better put it right back on or you may get written up by your manager. More about getting written up later…

Sam had been working at the Market for 15 years. He started out as a Courtesy Clerk which was just a glorified name for "box boy/girl. When he began working at the store at age 17, he never thought he'd grow up to be working at the very same store! Now, at age 32, he wondered why he never remembered thinking, *I wonder what I'll be when I grow up.* Maybe he should have questioned it. Sure, the pay was okay and there were medical and dental benefits, but he had to stand up all day and stay in one place day after day, hour after long hour. The only real thrill was that he knew he would get rotated around shifts. Getting a different check stand was just about the most exciting thing that could happen in the life of a checker!

What Sam really lived for were the people. Ah, yes! The people! Sam loved people. At least, he thought he did. However, some days he hated people. Take, for example, his least favorite regular customer, Lucille.

Lucille

Lucille was a really eccentric older woman in her 80's. Most people didn't know it, but she was one of the best concert pianists around. She taught piano for over 50 years and played in colleges, universities, and accompanied dance classes over half her life. She didn't live far from the market, about four blocks or so, and she lived alone. Lucille didn't drive anymore so she walked or took the bus everywhere she needed to go at the ripe old age of 88. Like fine wine, she was a vintage not to be forgotten.

Lucille wore three hats and very large, dark glasses. That's right, three hats! She frequently went to garage sales to buy hats, hats of all kinds. She started out with a scarf to keep her hair back, and then added a stocking cap for warmth, and on top of that she put on her wicker sun hat to keep out the sun, or rain. Usually rain since it was the Pacific Northwest after all. The weather determined the hat style she would choose but it didn't matter what the weather looked like, she always wore the dark glasses.

Every time Lucille entered the market, there was a (silent) red alert among staff. In fact, in some departments, like the Deli, anyone who was working the check stands would pick up the intercom and announce (in secret code) "I need a price check for a "hat" on check stand 2." This was the secret signal that Lucille had entered the building. You may wonder why the deli asked for a warning. It's pretty simple, really. They needed to get ready for her arrival, for her wrath, for her aura to be shown upon them! You see, Lucille liked everything EXACTLY how she wanted it. To the T!

Considering the adage, the customer is always right, Lucille demanded it. All she wanted were three chicken legs, and they had better be the ones on top. No, not the sexual position, but rather, in laymen's terms, on top of the pile of chicken legs in the deli hot case. Lucille didn't want those precious little legs sitting in any grease. No matter how hard one tried to convince her that some of it was just good old fashioned chicken juice, she didn't want any of it! No how! No way!

Any seasoned deli worker who knew Lucille knew that you'd better be ready and waiting at the counter when her three hats come around the corner. If you were a new deli worker, have mercy on your soul! If you didn't know the score, you were about to find out!

Anytime Lucille approached the counter, you couldn't even see her. She was about 5 feet tall so you couldn't see her face, just her three hats. Her little face and glasses just peered up from below the rim and you'd think to yourself, run alien, run! What the heck is this?

In her matter-of-fact voice, you'd hear, "Hello? Hello? Is anybody here to help me? Hello! I need help!" Everyone in the deli came to attention and everyone came running. She'd say, "I don't need all of you, I just need one!" Like a bad joke, they'd all go back to what they were doing because it really only required one deli worker to wait on Lucille and the bravest one always stepped forward.

Cindy had been working in the deli for six years. She had two sons and had been divorced for over 10 years. Like Sam, Cindy loved people. She was a fairly pretty woman and loved the fact that she didn't look her age, which she contributed to her DNA. She didn't always eat right, definitely didn't drink enough water, and hardly exercised much since she stopped dancing. That's how she knew she must have good genes!

Cindy stepped up to the case and greeted Lucille. Nobody who worked at the market knew, but Cindy and Lucille went way back. Lucille used to play piano for one of Cindy's dance classes many years ago. Cindy was not afraid of her; in fact, she liked and respected her and knew she was one hell of a piano player.

"Hi Lucille, how are you today? Would you like your usual order?" Cindy asked with a smile.

"Oh, hello Cindy. Yes, three from the top and I'll be back in a minute. I need to go get a few more items." Lucille chimed.

"Ok Lucille. I'm off in about 15 minutes, but I'll let them know this little white bag in the hot case is yours, ok?" Cindy replied.

Lucille, in her old age, was getting pretty forgetful as we all tend to do, if we are lucky to live as long as Lucille. An hour passed and the deli cases were cleaned out and closed down. Lucille was still in the store. Sam, who was the PIC (Person in Charge) every other Wednesday night and had to work the closing shift every two weeks, was called to the deli. Sam heard over the intercom, "PIC to the deli, please, PIC to the deli." Sam ran back to the deli thinking a pipe had broken or one of the clean-up kids had hurt themselves but there stood Lucille. She was demanding her chicken legs and asking why the deli closed so dang early.

"Why can't they stay open longer?" She asked.

Sam was frantically running all over the deli looking for her chicken. He had no idea where they put her scrumptious little morsels. He knew one thing however, that come Hell or high water he was going to find them! He searched everywhere; the walk-in where the refrigerated supplies were kept and the hot case that had been cleaned and closed. Then, lo and behold, he saw a little white bag sitting inside the closed down salad case where the salads were covered each night.

The case was still fairly loaded and there it was between the covered pasta salad and the Tabbouleh. It had Lucille's name scrawled across it with a little smiley face. *BINGO! Praise the Lord! Jackpot!!* Sam silently recited every blessing he could think of in a split second because in that moment he knew he would not have to deal with Lucille's wrath, had he not found that little white bag. She terrified him.

"Here it is Lucille, all safe and tucked away for you." Sam handed her the bag over the countertop.

Lucille looked up and said, "Thank you so much. Please document that I really would like the deli to stay open one more hour." She turned to walk out the door.

Sam grabbed a piece of paper and pretended to jot down Lucille's request. He briskly threw it away once he was sure her three hats had completely cleared the store.

Whoever said the customer is always right should be discredited. What they should have said was that without a customer, you have no business. Without a business, you have no jobs for yourself, or for anybody. So, treat those folks like gold because if you do them right, they will tell everybody they know. If you do them wrong, they will also tell everybody they know, plus a thousand more including their dogs, cousins, aunts, and uncles….you get the point.

Sam always bent over backwards for everyone in every job he'd ever had. That was probably why he was awarded PIC of the month and employee of the month. In the grocery business, employers like to give a little incentive. A morale-booster, if you will. Somewhere, someone said not to worry about giving people a raise every 3-6 months, or discounts on food, or things they could really use. Instead, give them a parking spot close to the main entrance so they don't have to walk as far as everyone else.

Sam had gotten every award possible in the grocery business and had never actually used that coveted parking spot because "walking is good exercise and God knows when I'm in that little check stand, I'm not going anywhere." Yes, change for the till was brought to him; water was brought to him…oh yeah, they let you have water.

.

Unexpected Connections

Well, how are you this morning? Did you find everything you were looking for?" Anna asked the next very handsome customer to come through her check-out lane. Anna was one of the newer employees at the market. She had not yet become jaded enough to lose her beautiful smile and cheerfulness or her mind from waiting on customer after grumpy customer for years on end.

"Yes, I did, thanks," answered the handsome man with a beard wearing a suit and a bow tie. "In fact, I got more than what I came in for." He hurriedly unpacked his basket because he was running late for work but didn't want to appear rude. The questions continued.

"Well that's great! Do you have your discount card?" Anna asked politely.

"No," the handsome man answered abruptly.

"Would you like to apply for one today?" Anna asked.

"Can I just do that online? I'm in a hurry." He said.

"Yes, you can. Here is my card with my company number on it. If you enter that number you will receive a 15% discount on your next purchase with us." Anna smiled.

Mr. Handsome was getting irritated. All he wanted to do was buy his juice, his half-tuna, half-egg salad sandwich, and the cookies he threw in for his afternoon, well-deserved treat for working so hard. His plan was to eat the egg-salad sandwich for breakfast and the tuna sandwich for lunch. He began to wonder if he would ever go back to that market, especially if he was in a hurry. Too many questions!

"Look," he said. "I know you are just trying to do your job but I'm late for work and really need to get going."

Her smile turned upside down and her eyes got watery. The handsome man felt bad. He didn't mean to sound like a jerk and realized his impatience made him appear that way.

"You know what?" he said more calmly. "I don't care if I'm late for work after all. If it doesn't take that long, I'll apply for the discount card. It's free right?"

"Yes, great. It only takes a minute. Here is the form. You can add the company number there at the bottom." Anna pointed to the space on the form and her smile returned as she wiped the moisture from her eye. She hated that she cried so easily, especially at work.

Through the process of the transaction, they found out that growing up, they had lived just blocks from each other and their parents were life-long friends. They had also both lost their parents in the past year. They exchanged phone numbers and decided they would have coffee soon and talk. They would console each other and catch up on their lives. After all, misery loves company.

At the market, such meetings were a daily occurrence. People ran into old friends and made new ones. You remember that song, "make new friends, but keep the old, one is silver and the other's gold."

Wheelchair Games

The market was right across the street from the retirement home where Ruth Green and George Green lived, no relation, they were not married. In fact, they didn't even speak to each other nor did they like each other at all. For some odd reason, they would always go shopping on Monday. Neither Ruth nor George could walk very well, so they played this little game. One would leave the retirement home at about 11:30 and the other would leave at 11:35. That was when the fun began!

Since they both had to use a cane, it took them about 12 to 15 minutes to get across the street. The silly thing was that they would both walk on different sides of the street and enter through different doors heading slowly, but surely, to the one and only electric wheelchair cart in the store. If George got there first, Ruth would take her cane and start tapping the floor demanding she was there first saying, "…and what about politeness and respect to a lady anyway?" George would start yelling to the PIC on shift, "When is this dang store going to get another wheelchair cart?"

On one given day, Sam was in the front at the check-out stand checking the identification of someone who looked 15 years old trying to buy cigarettes. Right about that time, Ruth would enter through one door and George from the other. The race was on! Who was going to get the wheelchair first? As they approached the target, Sam turned just in time to see two canes fly up into the air like a duel. It reminded him of Arthur and Lancelot sword fighting, or Darth Vader and Luke Skywalker, except that Ruth and George could hardly lift their canes over their heads. They were causing a huge raucous! He was afraid someone would get hurt in this battle for the electric wheelchair cart! Sam rushed the young punk through the check stand and refused the boy his nicotine addiction. What happened next, nobody could have predicted.

Another elder, small in stature with bone-white hair holding a cane, quietly walked right up behind Ruth and George as they were bickering when suddenly he sat in the wheelchair cart and proceeded to drive away. Ruth and George were so busy fighting over the wheelchair cart that they did not even notice when it was gone. Sam began to laugh really hard which caught their attention. They stopped in their tracks when they realized that the wheelchair cart was gone and the looks on their faces were priceless! Ruth and George looked at each other, then glanced at Sam, and started to laugh even louder than anyone else who may have been watching the whole scene unfold. They realized, even in their 80's, that the joke was on them. It was like one of the famous Beetle's songs, "…there is no time for fussing and fighting, my friend."

Sam thought it served them right. After all these years why couldn't they just go have tea together, or a shot of port, or whatever you drink when you're old and pissed off at the world? They were both alone and their family members never even came to visit them. So, there you have it! Ruth and George, Mutt and Jeff, Porgy and Bess…unbelievable! Why couldn't they just get along?

No sooner did the thought cross Sam's mind, Ruth and George scooted their way to the food court where they treated each other to a doughnut and a cup of coffee. They remained good friends ever since.

Wet Cleanup On Aisle Four

Some days were more challenging than others at the market. Some days went by with absolutely no unforeseeable incidents; but usually that was not the case. Every day had some sort of challenge. There was one day when Sam was not prepared for what lay ahead, or maybe he was.

The coolers at the market were very, very cold but they kept breaking down. The owner said that if they went out on him one more time he'd buy all new coolers throughout the entire market. Well, that meant thousands of dollars because there were about fifteen very large coolers in the store and they weren't cheap. There were coolers for the dairy products, and for the meat, the frozen vegetables, frozen fruit, juice, ice cream, etc. However, the meat cooler seemed to go out constantly, which was crazy because it kept very expensive products from spoiling.

Steak and roasts can be worth upwards of $35 - $40 bucks a pop! So, when the meat cooler went out, everybody panicked. Sam got the call, "wet cleanup on aisle four!" which he dreaded because that was the meat aisle. Wet clean-up meant; bring a mop, bring lots of mops, and a bucket full of soapy water. Dry clean-up meant; get your brooms ready. Of course, the worst mess happened in the wine and beer section. All the liquid and broken glass makes quite a mess! If it were possible to get a buzz from the alcohol fumes that would be an added bonus, but that never happened. It never failed when a bottle of wine broke on the floor, a passing customer would always say, "Get me a straw and I will take care of that mess for you!"

"Wet cleanup on aisle four!" The announcement blasted again over the intercom.

Sam, on his way to the disaster, took with him a couple of carts with ice in the bottom to load everything up from the meat cooler so that hopefully it wouldn't spoil. It took two courtesy clerks to help move, clean, and take care of the mess. Usually, right before the cooler went down, it started playing music. That's right, it was the fans (Sam thought) hitting its blades together but it sounded like a song. Clank, clank, do da clank, de clank...it started out slow and then got faster and faster and until it got really loud just before breaking down. You could not even think over the noise it made!

Sam had been through this many times so was somewhat prepared for what he was about to encounter. That particular day he had a different wet-cleanup on aisle four, however. That time it meant something else. Matt, the meat department manager, had once and for all decided to find the root cause of the giant freezer problem. He had already moved all the meat out of the case to another cooler and dove head first into the guts of the monster. He ran a hose into the beast in an attempt to defrost it because the motor had all kinds of ice-build on it. What happened was that the hose had sprung a leak and "Ol' Faithful" was shooting water up to the ceiling, flooding everything and everyone around! The flooding originated from the meat department, into the paper aisle and out from the freezer, of course. Luckily the paper towels were packaged nicely in their plastic pouches, but the Kleenex and matches weren't so lucky. Spoiled merchandise meant lost revenue.

By the time Sam got back to aisle four, it was clean, but the other end was a disappointing situation. One customer was completely drenched and trying to help another customer up off the floor; she had fallen! Right smack in the middle of all of it was a younger guy screaming and panicking. *Isn't that just great!* Sam thought. *Ol' Faithful right here in the market! Let's all just take a shower in it and celebrate life!* His inner sarcasm was extremely flippant. It's a good thing nobody could hear his thoughts.

Sam, once again, could not believe his eyes. He did his best to recall his safety training. What needed to happen first, second, third, etc. was rolling through his mind at lightning speed. Should he help the lady who had fallen first, would she need medical attention? Was she hurt? Sam was trying to remember the first aid class he had taken months ago. She wasn't bleeding, she was breathing, and she was crying…but was she in pain? He quickly made an assessment of the situation; there was water on the floor, so he looked around for any electrical cords or outlets around. Could she have been shocked? Oh, wait a minute, she was laughing! She was ok! *Whew*! Sam released the breath he'd been holding in from the adrenaline pumping through his body.

Her really high heels and clumsiness didn't help the situation. Her suit was completely soaked and Sam could see her nipples through her blouse. This was turning out to be better than a wet t-shirt contest during Spring break in Florida! It seemed like there would be no lawsuit but he still needed to get all the information written down just in case in the future she decided she broke her hip, or some nonsense, and then decide to sue.

One of the courtesy clerks rushed off to the back of the store for the incident report paperwork. It needed to be done as soon as possible so Sam politely asked the woman to wait. She complied and Sam was glad that was done! A bakery clerk was passing by on his way to the break room to get some more help and Sam asked him to grab a few more towels for the drenched customer. He also asked him to take the "hippie guy" to get him those free cookies from the free cookie jar in the bakery. "Better yet, take him by bulk foods and just let him graze there, thanks!" He was tired of him standing around gawking while he tried to attend to the woman in the wet, now transparent blouse.

Meanwhile, Matt the meat department manager, had turned off the water to the hose, collected the mop buckets, and escorted the people out of the affected aisles. Everyone was helping Sam keep things under control and needless to say, the floor on aisle four was incredibly clean! Once again, Sam had proven why he was PIC of the month.

Sam In Love

Sam had never been married. He was about 6'1" and not a bad looking guy. He was a little on the skinny side, drank way too much coffee, and lived alone in a one-bedroom apartment. About five years ago, he had fallen in love with Barb, who worked in the Deli.

You see, when you work somewhere for 40+ hours a week, it's not uncommon to fall in love with somebody else who works there. It could be a co-worker, a delivery person, or a sales rep. Life in the market is the center of your Universe, your womb, your bubble. Heck, you spend half or more of your life at the job site and it seems like everything, besides sleeping and showering, happen there.

Sam wanted to have outside interests like biking, hiking, or skiing, or pretty much anything else at that point in his life, but by the end of his shift he was too drained emotionally, physically, and mentally. He didn't have any energy left for any sort of outdoor activity, or for anyone special, but he always dreamed of Barb. He made a point to make multiple trips back and forth to the deli whenever he could during his shifts. However, it never failed that when Barb would wait on him, he would hear over the intercom, "PIC to the front, PIC to the front!" That meant he had to get back to work and continue his break later.

Crap! He thought to himself. *Well, I didn't want that mac and cheese anyway. I just wanted Barb to look at me with those gorgeous, green eyes and make me feel special, if only for a moment.* The sad truth was that Barb asked everyone she served how they were doing and what she can get for them because it was her job. She didn't really pay Sam any special attention.

Sam left the deli to attend the needs of the front of the store only to find an irate shopper who couldn't believe that last week she had spent an additional $.10 for a product that was now on sale! When Sam took a deep breath to prepare for battle, he said to himself, *"Remember, the customer is always right, so here goes…"*

"Hello, my name is Sam. How can I help you today?"

"Oh, hello Sam, my name is Hildegard Smith and I bought this orange juice here last week for $.10 more than what it costs today."

"Well, Ms. Smith…" Sam began.

"Mrs…I'm married," she retorted.

"Ok, Mrs. Smith. It may be on sale this week. Let me check the ad. Also, I know the growers have had a rough season, lots of rain, hurricanes in Florida, so the price sometimes fluctuates. But, I'll tell ya what I can do. I'll refund you the $.10 so you can be on your way."

Since Sam was thinking that the customer was always right, he didn't want to argue over a measly ten cents. Not Sam. This was what he had to leave Barb's eyes for? *Unbelievable!* Another satisfied customer.

By the time he took care of Mrs. Smith and got back to the deli, Barb had already gone on her break. Sam thought to himself that this had been going on for five years now. It must not be in the stars. It must be an omen. Barb will never want to be with a grocery store PIC. His mind trailed off while he grabbed a cup of coffee from the espresso stand and headed to the break room.

Typical break rooms are pretty dirty and only a few people ever bother to clean up after everyone else. It was the same people in there day after day, usually the full-timers. The same people sat in the exact same seats at the exact same times of the day, eating the same food day after day. You could almost set your watch by it. We called them the department head honchos, the decision makers, the "cream of the crop," the "we-got-it-together" folks or the "chosen ones."

It was surprising they were still alive when you think about it. Most of them lived on Coca-Cola, chips and fried potatoes from the Deli. You'd never see a vegetable graze anywhere near their lips, let alone good 'ol' H2O. Managers beware: you can't be part of this club if you eat well and don't have some really juicy gossip about your co-workers!

The break room was a place where employees could go to let out all of their anxieties from work, home, and all of it. If someone sat in the break room from 9 to 5 with a tape recorder, it was highly doubtful you would hear anything positive. Japan has Tai Chi rooms, Mexico has a place for siestas, here in good 'ole America we have our break rooms! (A.k.a. Bitching Rooms)

There were two sections of the break room in the market. One was a big, long room with a long table down the middle with chairs all around it, an old coffee maker, and one old microwave. The other area was a room that opened out to the roof where all the smokers could fill their lungs with toxins. This was where Sam would definitely find Barb.

A lot of employees went to the roof for the view and fresh air, not only the smokers. It helped knowing that there was an open door up there so that hopefully one wouldn't get lung cancer from the second hand smoke. However, there was always that risk, without a doubt.

Sam strolled through the produce department to the back room filled with boxes and clutter. He ascended the very steep set of stairs and noticed his legs were very achy. When he got to the top of the stairs, he realized that he needed to start using his gym membership. He bought one last January as a New Year's' resolution to take better care of himself, but had not once used it. Now would be a great time!

He felt butterflies in his stomach as he paused on the landing to catch his breath. Maybe it was because he hadn't eaten anything and had just consumed a large cup of coffee. Sam gathered up his courage to attempt to talk to Barb while he walked down the dark corridor, passed the first break room where one lonely employee was sitting and eating their lunch of Fritos and Coke. He thought to himself that this country has the most overweight, unhealthy people in the entire world!

He opened up the door to the smoke-room only to find it empty. He noticed that the ashtray was completely filled to the rim, but Barb was nowhere in sight. He was confused. Where was she, he wondered. The deli clerk said she was on her break and she always went there on her first break of the day. Maybe she had a quick errand to run? Was somebody at the deli misinformed?

Sam felt a slight feeling of relief and let out a big sigh, but he was still deeply disappointed. He could never seem to get his personal life in check. He felt very discouraged and headed back down the dark corridor, which seemed even darker now. His break was almost over. Suddenly he saw Barb coming out of the restroom. Great! What would he say now? Probably something really stupid like, "how did everything come out?" or "Did you know there's toilet paper hanging out of the back of your pants?" He decided to just say nothing instead of cracking a stupid joke. He held back, said hi, and watched her go down the stairs.

Instantly he headed into the men's room to go beat his head against the wall, or better yet, wash his face to collect himself to finish the rest of his shift. It felt like a very long day already.

Barb

Barb had worked in the deli for five years and truthfully, did not enjoy her job. Deep down inside, Barb didn't like herself. She never really knew her own father and he had never tried to get in touch with her. While she was growing up, her father never contributed financially to the family; an unfortunate, yet common situation in today's society. That was partly why she also disliked her step-father with a passion! He drank constantly and was abusive to her mother. She loved her mom a lot, but of course couldn't understand why she put up with such a rotten man.

Barb smoked, ate very poorly and never exercised, yet she was beautiful and behind her beautiful eyes was so much sadness. Her beauty increased 1,000-fold when she did smile. She had the kind of smile that "lights up a room" like a beacon from a lighthouse; she'd shine.

Sam would have loved to try to make her happy. Everyone would've loved to see Barb truly happy, but some people just aren't. It seemed to be her fate in the world. She made decent money working in the Deli for never accomplishing anything higher than a high school diploma. She had medical and dental insurance which she used a lot. Yep, she always had something "wrong" with her because she was a hypochondriac. One week she had a cold, the next week her eye hurt, the next it was her stomach, and on and on. It seemed, without a doubt, there was always something wrong. Maybe it was just to get attention or something to talk about. "What's up with you Barb?" "Why do you spend so much time at the doctors'?" These were common questions in the deli.

There was one doctor in particular with which she spent a lot of time. It was true that Sam was in love with Barb, but Barb was in love with her doctor. That's right! It's a sad and mixed up world, isn't it? Maybe that explained the frequent illnesses.

Laura and Greg

Laura was around 58 years old and had worked in the Deli for twenty years. Her husband was, more or less retired and Laura was a workaholic. She talked about her husband from time to time, but no one had ever seen him before. Nobody knew why. She was definitely one of the hardest working women you'd ever meet.

Going into the break room on one particular day, her complaint was a simple one. She had just come from the women's restroom where someone (with a seemingly very poor diet) had just relieved themselves, stunk up the bathroom, and didn't have the smarts, brains, or courtesy to light a match or use the provided room deodorizing spray. Or, they could have just left the door open for a few minutes to air it out. Laura was pissed! (No pun intended)

She walked into the break room and shouted, "Ok, who was the last person to come out of the women's restroom? Never in all my days have I smelled such a foul odor in my life! How is anyone expected to go in there after that? I want to know!"

Nobody said a word. Nobody. Everyone was so dumbfounded that Laura would even talk about such a forbidden topic! Laura didn't have a problem with it. In fact, telling dirty jokes and pinching the young men who worked there in the bum, was all part of Laura's daily routine. She meant no harm, but was a bit out of control and she figured that nobody would ever do anything about it anyway. She was a hard worker and had been there such a long time that she got away with a lot. She was above the rules. In fact, she made her own rules because she did half or more of the deli department managers' job so they were never going to fire her if anyone complained. Who ever said women don't sexually harass men?

Sam overheard Laura's rant about the smelly restroom and realized that he has just witnessed Barb coming out of it. He smirked and went back to the check stand.

There are some people who are born to work. From the minute they take their first breath they are ready to go to work for somebody, or for themselves. Who they work for is irrelevant, they were worker bees. Laura had worked ever since she could remember. At the age of ten, she had her own paper route. Then, she graduated to babysitting for $.50 an hour until she turned 17 when she went to work in a grocery store. She bagged and delivered groceries, worked in the meat department wrapping meat, the bakery, and then the Deli.

Laura took care of all the ordering of products, gave a wink to the deli department manager if she thought someone was worth hiring upon being introduced to them, and basically took over if the manager was out for any reason. Actually, Laura had been in charge for quite some time so if one really wanted to make it in the deli, they better make sure they kiss Laura on the fanny at least once a week or better yet, allow her to pinch theirs. One had to put up with all her dirty jokes and above all else, never say anything bad about her, or she would make their life a living Hell, seriously!

You see, Laura loved and hated her job. What she really wanted to do was retire, but since her husband didn't work she had to and when she wasn't working at the market 40-hours a week, she was at home trimming trees, moving gravel, painting her deck; she just couldn't sit down unless it was to have a cup of coffee and a smoke. In fact, when she was on a break she usually stood up. She said that if she stopped too long and stayed in one place she may as well take a nap. That was something Laura had never done – taken a nap! She didn't believe in sleeping during the day, not even if she was sick.

That's another thing, Laura never missed a day of work in her life and if someone else called in sick and she got the call, you'd hear her say, "Well, if you're not bleeding profusely or throwing up all over the place then I suggest you better at least try to make it to work." A lot of people had been convinced to go to work even though they felt like crap.

Laura believed everyone should be like her. That meant that if you're a girl then you need to have short hair. Long hair just got in the way of work. You also needed to wear shoes just like Laura's because they are the only ones on the market (for $90) that keep your legs from getting tired. It's an occupational hazard, and anyone who works in a market will tell you that you will be on your feet all day. It goes with the territory.

At the market, everything was ordered on Monday. On this particular Monday, Laura went into the back room and came out saying, actually yelling, "Those dang beer distributors have done it again! They stacked all the dang back stock in front of the deli dry goods and I can't see what I need to order. I guess I'll just have to go manually move cases of beer myself!"

The martyr headed off to complain to the PIC. That day Greg was the lucky PIC and had worked at the market for ten years. He ran back to help Laura move the beer boxes. Greg ordered all of the imports and even though he did drink some beer, the imports were way too expensive for thrifty Greg to drink. Every once in a while the beer reps give him a free bottle or a six-pack, but you'd never see Greg going through the check-out with anything more than a $6.99 six-pack. Greg would rather spend his money on a big screen TV, Mariner tickets, or baseball caps. He had 52 baseball caps! Oh, and haircuts. He liked to sport a military buzz.

Greg was not a bad looking dude, very thin, but his younger brother Jason, who also worked at the market in the produce department, had every man, woman, and child smiling at him because Jason was gorgeous! That's right, knock-down, bend-your-neck-to-look-at-this-one HOT! He had the kind of lips that made women just want to kiss and suck and bite! He also had a very amazing smile as well as a great rear end! Basically, he had the perfect body.

Jason rarely had time for girls. Like his brother, he was a Mariner baseball fan and an avid snowboarder who would rather be hanging out with his buddies than be in a full-time relationship. However, he couldn't seem to get away from women; young, old, tall, short, blonde, brunette, or any type. He also had been working at the market for ten years and in that time, had many a proposition over the bananas. Hell, you could find women asking dumb questions like, "Why are the red peppers red?" Or maybe they were just commenting on the price of blueberries. Most of the time Jason was very friendly and just answered their stupid questions, but sometimes they would get pretty annoying.

One day, Jason was over by the potatoes stacking them in neat piles, making them look all pretty, when he felt a pinch from behind. *God!* He thought. *This isn't even funny. Now they're going to start touching me?* This time, it wasn't a woman. No folks! This time Jason was being harassed by a man, an old man!

Jason was pissed but he said nothing to his manager about it. He requested a break from Dave, his manager, and high-tailed it to the break room. He went to the smoker's section where he could ponder what had just happened over his sixth cigarette of the day even though it was only 10:30 a.m. He went upstairs, through the back hall and into the smoke room where he found Cindy from the deli. Nobody at the market knew it yet, but Cindy and Jason had been lovers, friends, bike-riding partners, meal companions, and more. Jason was 27 and Cindy was 40. For the last six months Jason had been so happy whenever he saw Cindy, he could almost cry.

Jason had been really quiet about their friendship because he didn't want anyone to find out about them, let alone what just took place down amongst the sweet potatoes. He told her to come closer. Cindy thought, *oh, my! He's going to kiss me at work.* That was a risk he had never taken, but instead he said very quietly, "That old geezer just pinched me on the floor in the produce department – in broad daylight!"

Now Cindy was pissed! She could tell Jason wasn't very happy about the event. He'd had men come onto him before, because he had such a pretty face, but he wasn't known for sticking up for himself.

"Do you think he's still in the store?" Cindy inquired.

"I don't know." Jason said.

"Describe him" pleaded Cindy.

Jason wished he hadn't said anything. He knew Cindy was brave enough to go give that guy a piece of her mind. Remember, she was the only one in the deli that waited on Lucille, the hat lady. She wouldn't think twice to go and say something to the old pervert!

Jason started making up some excuse that he had seen him leave before he came up for his break but it didn't matter anyhow. Oh yes it did matter, Cindy said that man violated him, he touched him without permission, he did the unthinkable, he touched HER man. You see, Cindy knew Jason was kind of homophobic and Cindy had almost been raped years ago. This event was bringing up all kinds of issues for both of them and together they would get through it because deep down, even though Cindy was too old for Jason and he knew they had no future, he wanted to get married and have kids someday.

Cindy had already done both so that was not what she was looking for but they truly loved each other and they had a great time together when they were alone. They had the best sex they had ever had when they were together. Jason had not been with very many lovers so she didn't have much to compare to but Cindy, at age 40, had already been divorced for about 13 years. She'd had her share and it's true what they say, summer, winter, spring, or fall whatever that saying is, rings true. He saw a lot of older men out there with younger women, and older women with younger men.

In Cindy's eyes, Jason was everything she'd ever wanted; funny, kind, handsome, and yes, mature! His age had nothing to do with maturity. She just felt incredible whenever she was around him and he felt awkward, like people were staring and maybe even wondering if she was his older sister, or mom. All of Jason's friends gave him a hard time because most of them, heck, all of them didn't even have a girlfriend, let alone a woman friend. Cindy thought they were jealous, but this would be the final straw that would eventually break Jason and Cindy up.

After a two year on-again/off-again relationship, he had started lying to his friends that he was going out for a bike ride and really just riding over to Cindy's house for dinner and a quickie. She found out about him lying to slip out and they slowly dis-connected from each other because, remember, they had fallen in love. They stayed friends and to this day still remember the dinners, the great sex, the trips, the bike rides, and the fun.

Peter and Joe

The produce department was an interesting place full of great colors, a wide variety of vegetables; some organic, some not. The displays were intricate and every market tried to out-do the other with the freshest, fanciest displays. The little and big red tomatoes were all stacked like balls being racked up for pool; carrots were arranged in a semi-circle, each one strategically placed on top of the other; the lettuce was trimmed, never wilted...fresh, fresh, fresh! You could feed a small country with what was thrown away in the largest grocery store, but luckily this market had Peter.

Peter was about 75 years old and was reported to be a millionaire. He even raised his own pigs! Peter always had on old, torn, worn-out dirty clothes but was very friendly and polite, always. He was the kind of man you wanted to give a makeover to because it was obvious that underneath all that filth was a handsome, strong man (and supposedly rich).

He came in about three times a week, sometimes every day at 6:30 a.m. to back up his little pick-up truck to the loading dock and pick up those unsightly tomatoes with the black spots on them, or the lettuce that was just a tad bit too wilted for display, and of course lots and lots of brown bananas which he gave to Cindy from the deli. She liked to freeze them to use in smoothies or banana bread to give to, you guessed it, Peter! He always came by the deli in the morning and asked Cindy if there was any leftover chicken from the night before. Cindy got the night time closers to put just a few pieces away for Peter before they would throw the rest out. That's right! Throw it out!

26

On one particular morning around 6:30 a.m., Peter was nowhere to be found. Where was he? 7:00 rolled around...7:30, still no Peter! Everyone was getting really worried because normally you could set your watch by Peter's schedule. Cindy called Peter's neighbor because two years prior Peter had a heart attack and was lying on his kitchen floor until someone found him. Peter didn't believe in phones, running water, or electricity, so Cindy called and found out he was in the hospital but not because of a heart attack this time. He had been out drinking the night before and plowed his truck into a tree, wrecked his truck pretty good, and was taken to the hospital to get check out. He was ok, but he was in trouble because he didn't have a license and never had one! Oh Boy!!

Cindy couldn't believe the story, but in a way she could, knowing Peter. She called the hospital to see if there was anything she could do. He asked her to come get him, but to first stop by his house and get the strawberry-shaped cookie jar to bring with her. Peter had a bill to pay at the hospital and every cent he had was in that strawberry cookie jar; thousands and thousands of dollars because Peter didn't believe in banks either. Peter didn't believe in much, he had never been married and didn't have any children. No one knew who would get his land or his money when he died; probably the Goodwill or the Humane Society.

Cindy loved Peter like her own Dad who was already deceased and she would've done anything for him, just like she would do anything for the janitor, Joe. Joe had been a janitor for 35 years. He was approaching 69 years old. He, like Laura, was one of the hardest working people at the market. Joe had grey hair, thick glasses, and didn't really stand up straight anymore. He was slightly overweight, but not obese. He always wore the same striped shirt and khaki pants.

Joe started his shift at 7:30 p.m. checking and restocking the bathroom, going around and removing all of the black smudges on the floor with his own foot, rubbing them until they were gone while cursing all the women who wore those cheap high heels and boots, and the kids with their black-soled sneakers.

In general, Joe never said much and just went about his business. He'd say hello to everybody; his employer, customers, staff, and especially Cindy in the deli. Cindy worked all shift openings, closings, and middle-of-the-day, so she got to see just about everybody. One night, Joe confided in

Cindy that he was going to need heart surgery. Cindy was scared for him. She had already lost her dad and she would just freak out if anything happened to Joe. She decided to turn her fears into encouragement and make it a point to tell Joe for two weeks straight that he was as strong as an ox and no little heart surgery was going to knock him down.

Joe also had that sleep disorder where you forget to breathe so he had to go to bed with oxygen running into his nose. Anyway, Cindy was afraid, but he would never know it. The week before his surgery, Cindy told Joe that he would get all the chicken he wanted after the surgery. But, she knew darn well that he needed to clean up his diet starting with eliminating fried chicken for a while. She started saving him some leftover salads with plenty of veggies in them, but knew he would have nothing to do with them. He called it "rabbit food" and said, "Thanks anyway, but no thanks!"

Joe was sweeping the floor and getting ready to buff it like he did every night when he heard the PIC's voice, "Joe, intercom 2 please." Someone had locked their keys in the car and left the car running. Joe high-tailed it to the parking lot just in time to witness the car engine starting to overheat. It was a 1973 orange VW bus and the 21 year old outside of his van was screaming, "Do something, do something!" Joe rarely said a bad word about anyone but he was thinking, *well, you dumb ninny, this wouldn't be happening if you hadn't left the ignition on with the keys locked inside!*

The fire department was called and everyone inside the store was out watching the young man's first car, his pride and joy 1973 cherried-out camper pop-top VW van catch on fire! Cindy felt really bad for the young man and hoped that Joe the Janitor wasn't going to drop down dead right there in the parking lot from all of the excitement. People were running from across the street, from the retirement home, from all directions like it was the fourth of July. It seemed the entire neighborhood came to watch the flames and the fire trucks. First, the firefighters had to get the spectators under control. Joe was yelling like no one had ever witnessed, for everyone to get the heck back and let the firefighters do their job.

He was getting really pissed off but no one was listening and then before Cindy's very eyes, Joe hit the parking lot asphalt. Before she could blink an eye, a firefighter was doing CPR on Joe with three others while another half dozen more had surrounded the vehicle and successfully put out the fire. The whole back end of the VW Van, where the engine was, had burnt to a crisp. Joe was coming to. It had been one exciting night at the market and everyone concurred that is was the most eventful day in that neighborhood in a long time.

Meanwhile, two sixteen year olds in the store were running out the side door with their arms full of stolen beer. They thought nobody would notice with all of the commotion outside, but they were wrong. Greg, the import-beer delivery guy, spotted them and before anyone could say *supercalifragilisticexpialidocious*, he was running after them, yelling for back-up from Steve, the new checker and anyone else who wanted to go for a quick 100-yard sprinting dash around the back of the store. Greg was yelling at Cindy to call the cops.

Great! She thought to herself, *this just doesn't get any better.* Firemen and paramedics were called for Joe, and now the cops were being called for a couple of opportunist thieves! Cindy thought, *dang, I wish I had a popcorn machine! This is turning into quite a show and I could've made some extra money on the side by charging admission!*

Greg and Steve tried to catch up with the hooligans, but they came back empty-handed. At that point, Joe was being put onto a stretcher. He was ok, but a little tired from it all. Nonetheless, they took him to the hospital to get checked out anyway. His surgery would be prolonged another month because of the incident. He needed to gain all of his strength back first.

The VW Van was a total loss. The day resulted in one heartbroken young man, one not-so-heartbroken older man, and two teenagers sitting somewhere having a good 'ole time with two cases of Heineken.

When Joe finally went in for his surgery, everything went really well. Cindy circulated a card around the store for everybody to sign and took it up to the hospital. She even snuck in a piece of fried chicken, which put a big smile on Joe's face. She was the only one out of 75 employees to visit him. Joe always knew that girl was special to him, and vice versa. In another life, they probably would have been related, or lovers, or something.

The human body has an outstanding ability to heal and Joe was back to work exactly four weeks after his surgery. He even pulled his shirt up and showed Cindy the scar that ran from the top of his chest cavity between his nipples, down to his belly button like a zipper on a coat. They had split him open, but he was back buffing the floors and feeling better than ever in no time.

Six months later, Joe fell, or rather slipped on some grease on the deli kitchen floor which to this day, messed up his shoulder forever. He was ready to retire the following year, and boy was he ready! He deserved to retire. No more cleaning up stinky messes in the bathrooms, no more bulbs to be changed, cars to unlock, dirt, scum, or filth of any kind to clean up. Yep! Joe was going north to visit his brother in Ketchikan, Alaska to hook the "big one" and hopefully find some peace of mind. Cindy would miss him desperately, but she was happy for him.

People come and go a lot in the grocery business. They always seemed to hire new help in the summertime when there's more people passing through. Come fall and winter, most of those new hires were students so they took off to go back to college once school started again. It always gave the market a new shot in the arm to have those unseasoned newcomers, the greenhorns, in the store. Most of the regular patrons didn't like it. They wanted to see old familiar faces, not new young ones. It made them feel uneasy sometimes.

Mandy

Mandy gave him the sweetest of the sweetest smiles and said, "I am so sorry Hun, hand me over those canisters and your two shots are coming right up. They're on the house!"

Now there is something you need to know about Mandy. With all her years of customer service experience, she could change any bad situation into a good one. Her motto was, *kill them with kindness.* She smiled again and surprisingly, the angry customer was handing her the empty canisters and smiling back. He was getting his coffee for free and didn't care if he would be five minutes late for his appointment. He was getting something for free!

Something else about Mandy was that she did have her favorite employees, customers, and friends and they were always getting something for free or half off. The market owners know full well and didn't care. They didn't mind because Mandy was like the Goodwill Ambassador to the market. She would give directions to everybody and anyone in the store. She would smile her pretty little smile every day and in every way to everyone. It made people's day a whole lot brighter.

That level of customer service is almost unheard of nowadays. Mandy had gone as far as to take money out of her own purse. If one of her faithful customers forgot their money at home and they just ran out of milk and toilet paper and boy, they would be in big trouble if they didn't return home with that toilet paper! (No pun intended) Mandy would save the day!

Despite her cheery disposition, nobody realized that she had been battling her own health problems for the past five years. First, the doctors told her everything was ok. Then, they called her and said she needed to come back in for more tests. Back and forth, back and forth…but still she continued to smile despite her incessant worry. She was an inspiration to everyone. Cindy from the deli had known Mandy for about 25 years. A long time ago they both worked a summer for a local crab processing company. They stood in buckets of hot water in rubber boots so the heat came up and kept them warm. The facility had to be kept just above freezing to keep the crab fresh. Crab goes bad fast in warm buildings. Mandy was the senior worker who took Cindy under her wing and showed her how to clean crab faster than anybody else except for, of course, herself. So, needless to say, Cindy and Mandy were longtime friends.

Cindy knew that Mandy wasn't well and she was worried just like she worried about Peter, the old guy who picked up the rotten produce. Cindy was a worrier. So was Mandy. It was something they both shared. They both had hearts of gold and didn't let anybody tell them different, although, they had their moments.

Both of their lives had been about serving and caring for others. Women like that in this world as we know it are hard to find. In this *me, me, me* society people like that stand out brighter than any shining star in the night sky. When Cindy was pulled back to the coffee stand one morning as she walked by, during a rare moment when Mandy didn't have a customer, she shared with Cindy that she had cancer and would have to go in for an operation. Cindy was devastated! Her mentor, confidante, and role model was sick and suddenly Cindy felt sick too. What could she do? What could she say other than hide her fears and give Mandy a big huge hug?

"You will get through this Mandy, you always get through anything! We both have. Just like years ago when we thought for sure we'd freeze to death standing in the cold, cold warehouse shaking crab." Cindy reassured her.

Mandy fought back the tears and fears and Cindy slowly walked away, her smile had changed to a frown and her tears were swelling up in those big, blue eyes of hers. She had a lump in her throat.

A few weeks later, Mandy went in for her surgery. They believed they got it all, but only time would tell. Everything went back to normal for the most part, but Cindy went on a warpath coaxing her hero to eat better, take better care of herself, and stop taking care of everybody else for a while. That would be the day! It was in their blood, like the rain in the clouds of the Pacific Northwest, and they would both go to their graves being who they were, putting others before themselves.

One of the things amongst many that Mandy and Cindy shared was their love for sugar. They both went through the bakery constantly looking for the fallen cake, the slightly overdone cookie that couldn't be put out in the case, anything sweet, and they would, inevitably, run into Carrie the bakery manager.

Carrie

Carrie had two adopted kids, but no husband. She made the most incredible cakes; wedding, birthday, graduation, you name it, she could do it! She could take a driver's license picture of someone's son or daughter and make a cake look exactly like it in honor of their rights of passage. Her wedding cakes were classic. Her most popular wedding cake was a three-tiered cake, cream-colored, with icing that resembled old lace with lilacs cascading down the edges and around the sides. She was an artist, a master of her craft, but her real specialty was making erotic cakes! That's right! Big huge breasts with huge nipples, penis's complete with pubic hair and scrotum and last but not least, the lower half of a woman filled with delicious cream custard! *God bless Carrie!* She could take any object for any occasion and make a cake to commemorate it.

She was very careful to hide the erotic cakes from the patrons at the market and they would never be displayed in the showcase of the bakery with the other homemade cookies, donuts, cupcakes, and petit-fours. However, word got around that Carrie could deliver such cakes and she made a lot of money on the side doing it.

Carrie was a large woman with a great big smile, but she started balding very early on, around 16. Maybe it was from hormones - premature female balding, who knows? While she was in the back, in the incredibly hot bakery kitchen, she wore a wig, just like a hat sitting on her head; she had a red fuzzy wig on. She was constantly tugging at it and of course everyone knew it was not her real hair.

The wig was not an expensive wig. Carrie spent her money on her kids which she loved to death! Like a lot of other women in the market, she had a big heart too. She lent money to people less fortunate than herself because she knew her worth and she had a huge heart. She made cakes more creatively than anyone anywhere and she loved her kids and they loved her. She knew that love was really all any of us needed.

Carrie had a really old station wagon that she used for most of her own cake deliveries. Before a wedding or a party, she had to set-up because she didn't trust anyone else to do it for her. On one occasion, she was running late to set-up a cake for a party and was walking around the corner of the bakery counter carrying the cake she had been working on for the past 24-hours. She saw a customer opening the donut case, which was made of glass, and he didn't realize that there was someone standing directly behind the door with a cart full of groceries. The glass door was about to hit the cart straight on! She was caught between a rock and a hard place!

She had the cake in her hands, so there was nothing she could do but walk as fast as she could and use her own body weight to block the impact. She was moving but couldn't get there fast enough. The glass door hit the cart and suddenly everybody was trying to get out of the way of the shattering glass. It was a huge glass door and the sound as it hitting the floor compared to that of a car crash!

Everyone came running to see what could have caused the sound of breaking glass, meanwhile Carrie managed to put down the cake but with all of the commotion of trying to run and stop the whole affair from happening, her wig had come off and she stood in the middle of the bakery, completely bald! It was a toss-up trying to figure out which was drawing the most attention; the broken glass door, or bald Carrie!

She picked up her cake and headed for the station wagon, knowing she was late. The clean-up call had been announced over the intercom, "broken glass clean-up or dry clean-up to the bakery please!" Two front-end courtesy clerks showed up and there was glass everywhere in the donut case and all over the floor. All of the donuts had to be thrown out! Luckily, no one was cut or injured but the customer getting the donut and the one pushing the cart looked like they were in a state of shock. However, what really had the clean-up crew puzzled was the mass of red hair lying on the floor! Carrie did not come back for her wig as she only lived two blocks from the store, so she would stop at home and get her spare wig before going to the party. The show must go on!

Back at the bakery, the wig was picked up and placed in a bag with a note that read, "Carrie, I found this on the bakery floor. Wanted to return it to you. Have a good day. -Mike, front-end courtesy clerk."

He held his breath while he tried as hard as he could not to say the wrong thing. As he finished writing the note, a customer was out front yelling for some assistance.

"Hello? Hello! Anybody there?" Someone shouted.

"Yes!" Mike said. "I don't work in the bakery, but what can I do for you?"

It was a little old man, about 80 years old, asking why he just couldn't buy two hot dog buns. Why did they always come in packages of 8 or 12? The packaged buns don't even match the number of hot dogs in a pack! Mike was explaining that he could buy a full package and freeze what he didn't use, but when he looked up the old man had vanished into thin air. Mike wondered if he'd imagined it.

There had been sightings quite often in the market, making some employees believe there were ghosts walking the aisles. There had been crazy sounds and movement in the market that was unexplainable. Cans had been known to fall off the shelves and packages of cookies opened with only one cookie gone. Mice had been spotted in the deli, but in the case of the cookie packages, they had been neatly opened, no chew marks and one or two cookies missing and put back on the shelf. Maybe it was a night stalker? Maybe an angry employee pulling a prank? Nobody knew. It was puzzling. If they had actually installed some real cameras at the market, maybe they would have solved the mystery.

Steve the Security Guard

Steve, the "so-called" security guy came in between 3:00 - 3:30 pm when the middle school up the street let out for the day. He was mainly there to protect the candy bars and pop that the kids come in to steal. Steve took his job very seriously. He was a very big guy, as most security guards are, and he walked around looking like he was shopping with one of those red booklets in his hand, but everybody knew he was the security guy.

He was former military with a crew-cut. He was discharged because he got into too many fights and he drank too much. That was a very deadly combination; authority, craziness, alcoholism...a nightmare waiting to happen! When he was through doing his policing of the store around 6:30 pm, he turned into Joe the Janitor's assistant. Steve had caught some people stealing beer before, but in the two years he'd been there, that had only happened once. It was Steve's amazingly creative idea to install cameras in the market.

It has already been mentioned that there were no cameras in the market, but that's only partially true. In the ceiling, there were black, round cylinders installed to look like cameras but they were actually just empty shells. The owner really wanted to install security cameras, but when he found out how expensive that would be, Steve came up with the idea to close early on a Sunday night, put the word out to the community that some minor repairs were being completed in the store, and that's when the camera-looking decoys were installed. Each aisle had a row of them in the ceiling, especially close to the beer and wine section.

The employees started a rumor with Mandy, in the coffee shop, and Laura in the deli, the two big mouths, that the store had finally gotten the much needed security system and then when the word hit the street, the idea was that theft would drop to nothing and the owner would have spent half the price of all those other stores with their fancy alarm systems. It would have been a good plan except for one huge mistake! Mandy and Laura were huge gossipers, but they couldn't lie to save their lives! They told everyone about the new "system" and in a short period of time, they more or less forgot to keep their very large mouths closed and everyone, of course found out that the cameras were fake! So much for that brilliant idea!

Steve was furious when he found out that everyone knew. It was an angle he never considered; a base he had not covered. Nonetheless, the owner from that day forward was always looking for a reason to let Steve go. He had put up with him coming to work with alcohol on his breath. He had put up with the fact that he never ever caught anyone stealing, even though inventory was always short. This mistake he couldn't blame sweet Mandy for, or hard working Laura! No, this was Steve's doing. He had not presented a clear picture of what would happen if their little deception was, in fact, discovered. It was no surprise to anyone when Steve was discharged of his duties as security guard.

Steve came walking down the aisle trying, as usual, not to bring attention to himself, which was funny since not many large 6'4" men adorned their heads with crew cuts anymore. He was nonchalantly whistling as he strolled down the aisles. Betty Johnson, the local tycoon wife, who everyone knew was getting Alzheimer's, had just rounded the corner with some greeting cards in her hand. Steve actually saw her slipping them into her purse and without hesitation, or any questioning what-so-ever, had her spread eagle on the floor, yes-on the floor! You would have thought she had just robbed every check stand and cleaned out all of the cash registers!

Betty was yelling at the top of her lungs, "STEVE! Get off me, you big thing!" Steve was yelling for back up like some FBI agent with the largest fugitive known to man. It was like she was one of America's most wanted. The owner, the department head of produce, and anyone in earshot was running to see the little 5'2" 62 year old woman being held down by 6'4" Steve and all because of a few greeting cards!

Steve was fired that very day. A letter was sent off to Betty and Tim Johnson with a thousand words of apologies and to let them know that Steve no longer worked at the market. His excessive use of force and his action in the matter was uncalled for and way out of line. Store management knew the situation and not only did they know Betty was just putting those cards in a safe, flat place in her purse, they wanted to give the Johnsons a gift certificate for $100. It was with the deepest, most sincere apologies that the letter went out, but it never got a response. Betty and Tim Johnson never again stepped foot in that market.

When the town heard of such poor treatment to dear old Betty, well, let's just say word of mouth travels fast in a town of 80,000 people. Some faithful customers who had shopped there for over 20 years actually stopped shopping there forever! Betty and Tim Johnson were very well known, powerful people in the community and even though they all knew Betty was stealing those cards, there was always, in fact, an exception to every rule. Betty was not a mentally healthy woman.

No one knew where Steve went. The last anyone heard from him he was working in a local bar as a bouncer for very little pay and all the booze he could possibly want. What a dangerous thought! Steve was the kind of man who fell in love with every woman he met. Anytime a new woman was hired at the market, who was half way decent looking, and who said hello to Steve within the first 48 hours, he would ask her out. He gained quite the reputation and women stayed away from him.

Steve was so aggressive that they were all quite scared by his approach, which was analogous to a lion stalking a lamb. However, what turned the girls off most was the fact that Steve sweat like a fountain and walked around with a little towel over his shoulder that was drenched within the first 10 minutes of his shift. No one knew for sure why he sweat so much. Maybe it was his metabolism, heat, hormones, who really knew? He'd gone to the doctor to find out why, but they had no idea, so life went on. Everyone was glad to see him go!

The Night Stockers

Have you ever had to go to the store in the middle of the night? Many markets are open 24 hours and usually at around 12:00 a.m., or 3:00 a.m. for smaller stores, you will see the night stockers. They are usually burley men, young and old, who can lift at least 100 pounds and come to work all wide eyed and bushy-tailed to tackle the huge job of restocking the shelves. They love their jobs because most of them are burned out day workers who really could not imagine working with the public any more. It's a constant job for them because when the products leave the shelves, it leaves a little hole or space. Presentation is everything, so the presentations are always changing and those spaces need to be filled up with more products.

New products were delivered to the market regularly and the store needed to always look fresh and clean or else no one would want to shop there. There were usually one or two people who were in charge of going through the store every day, scrutinizing every aisle. They made notes of what needed to be ordered; canned goods, dry goods; they usually broke it down into sections so that they weren't overwhelmed. Monday may be cereal inventory day, Tuesday the baking aisle, etc. Nowadays, everything is electronic. Inventory control software has been installed so that as items are scanned at the check-out, as stock gets low, it's automatically re-ordered.

Product placement is also very strategic. Have you ever wondered why the milk and the eggs are in completely different areas? It's so that you have to go up and down each aisle looking for them which forces you to look at all the products in between and hopefully temp you to throw a few additional items into your cart. The impulsive shopper is the foundation of the business. Many will start off with the little shopping baskets with the intention of only picking up a few things, but that quickly turns into additional cravings; chips, ice cream, and look, a new and improved toilet bowl cleaner! It's amazing what people buy on a whim.

On one given night, the stockers had assembled in the break room to talk about their game plan in anticipation for the arrival of the mighty load! Half asleep, they wondered who would be the lucky one to do the unloading. Usually they tried to rotate the task from one to the other, but sometimes who showed up determined who got chosen. Jeff, the largest stocker, had torn his shoulder rotator cuff playing soccer, so he wasn't there. Greg, the beer stocker, had decided to pull some extra hours and work graveyard since they earned more money for that shift.

Greg may have been small and thin, but give him a triple-shot mocha and he'd get half the load put away in a blink of an eye. They had a couple of greenhorns on the night crew and Greg was watching one of them lift the heavy boxes to the end of the truck where the pallet boards were waiting for help from one very small fork lift.

"Oh boy," Greg uttered.

They may be young and strong now but they'll be feeling it in about 30 years. Greg tried to give the younger guy some advice on the proper lifting technique but he wasn't having anything to do with Greg. An hour later, he was asking Greg if there were any back support belts around. Greg went and grabbed one with a little sinister smile on his face. The guy put it on and it gave some support and relief for a while but the damage was already done. The muscles were pulled and the greenhorn spent the rest of the shift complaining left and right with every move he made. Greg wondered why someone didn't shoot him and put him out of his misery! Heck, if they can do it to a lame horse, why not this kid? Greg went to get another cup of coffee. If he ate as much as he drank coffee he would be 30 pounds heavier.

One of the really important tools of a night stocker is the box cutter. If you don't have a good, sharp one you are in big trouble. The job would take twice as long and everyone would suffer because it's a real team effort. The boxes were unloaded from the trucks, stacked as high as safely as could be and the frenzy began. The boxes of product got opened up and assembled on the shelves as fast as possible.

It never seemed to fail that in the frenzy of cardboard, products, hands, knees, and legs, that something always got sliced that shouldn't. Usually it was the cereal boxes. You know when you go to open a box of cereal and it's sliced right across the top or a bag of sugar that seems to completely empty itself out on the floor when you pick it up? Most likely that's not a manufacturer defect, but one of the hasty night stockers getting just a little sloppy with the box knife. It is a real art to know how deep to press the knife to open the top of those big boxes as fast as you can without damaging the product inside.

Often times, someone gets cut. It's an occupational hazard. On one fateful night, when nothing seemed to be going right, Greg was going to the canned food aisle only to discover the greenhorn had drawn the box knife right across his thigh. He was bleeding everywhere! Greg jumped into action and called 911. He had the young guy lying on his back trying to prevent him from going into shock. Greg was shaking from drinking so much coffee, or maybe it was from seeing all of the blood. The cut looked pretty deep.

It was 4 a.m. and the ambulance seemed to be taking forever. Greg was trying to remember his first aid which he never thought in a million years would ever need to be put to the test. The class was over a year ago, but something told him, or something he saw on TV reminded him, that there's a main artery in the thigh and if he could remember where exactly it was, he could possibly apply some needed pressure to the wound and stop the blood, or at least slow it down.

By the grace of God, he found it and applied the pressure. The paramedics finally arrived and took over. Greg sat right down on the floor and started to cry. He was exhausted and in shock himself. He knew they still had half the load to finish in the back and his workers were falling apart. He had just saved this greenhorn's life, the paramedics confirmed it. They said he did everything right. He covered him up, kept talking to him to keep him conscious, found the artery and applied pressure to cut off the main blood flow. Greg was a hero!

Greg didn't have time to think about that now. In just two short hours, the coffee drinkers and donut munchers would be in the store and they needed to get those boxes off the floor and shelves stocked. They also needed to clean up the blood and disinfect the floors. He dug deep within himself, collected his thoughts and emotions, and stood up and declared his instructions to the rest of the crew.

"Ok, dudes. Let's hit it! We've lost precious time and we need to get out of here. It looks like he's going to be ok, so let's get back to work!" He took everyone over to the espresso stand for a round of mochas. Mandy had shown him how to make them, and then they were back in the saddle, getting ready for the ride of their lives.

The night stock crew were two men short; one was a no show and the other one injured and off to the hospital. They had three men left to accomplish the unthinkable. They somehow managed to unpack and stock six more aisles in just less than two hours, something that had never been done as long as anyone could remember. It was astonishing! When the store opened up that morning, the story of Greg's heroic deeds spread through the store like wildfire thanks to Mandy and Laura. Stories get changed, however. It's the nature of gossip and this event was no exception. It varied from the greenhorn nearly cutting off his leg to Greg completely passing out at the sight of all the blood. Of course, neither one was true, but when it's word of mouth then the best storyteller tends to exaggerate just to throw some extra color into the already exciting story. That's life at the market.

The Greenhorn

Life is full of lessons and each new day brings a chance to learn, experience new things, and to grow. The market is like a small city. It's got a mayor (the owner), a police force (security guards), doctors and nurses (anyone who has completed CPR and first aid training), babies, new hires, seniors, and anyone who has been there longer than ten years. It's like a little civilization complete with all the craziness, anarchy, and politically incorrect (or correct) atmosphere. If you want to learn about life quickly, go to work at a market.

The greenhorn survived the whole ordeal. The cut in his leg healed up with a nasty scar, and when he was ready to go back to work. The owner thought it would be better for him to be taking care of those wild shopping carts out in the parking lot than to be a night stocker. Boy was he ever wrong! Some people are just destined to have an easier life than others, but the greenhorn was not one of them. He went back for about a week, and in that one week, he learned how to stack at least 50 carts in a row, how to pull them all in the rain, and how to lose control of all of them completely wiping out three customer's cars while they were shopping inside giving their hard-earned money to the market that employed 75 employees!

The market owner had to pay for the repairs of those cars and one of them was a brand new Jaguar! Why those carts couldn't have hit three old, used cars looking like they were fresh from Hawaii, you know those island cars full of rust that cost somewhere between $300 - $500, we'll never know.   Oh no, it had to happen to the brand new, expensive car! Greenhorn had just gotten all the carts together when he bent down to pick up a quarter. Yes, a quarter! By the time he looked up, they had all gotten away from him like a snake winding down a concrete walkway. The parking lot was on a steep hill and the carts sideswiped three cars on the way down the hill, clanking and scattering all over the place on the way down.

The greenhorn was on a 90-day probationary period and the owner felt that this guy just had the worst luck. He didn't want to be part of it. Everyone else felt really bad for him, but when an employee has cost you over $30,000 and hasn't even been working four months, the writing's on the wall.

Speaking of walls, what is with those people who take the time to always put graffiti on the front, side, and back windows, walls, and doors of markets? Did they paint and draw on their bedroom walls as kids and never get disciplined for it? Or, were they just not being heard or listened to and became angry and mentally ill? Poor Joe spent a fair amount of time cleaning, re-painting, re-cleaning, and re-painting all of the great little messages from "f*** you" to some gibberish no one but the person who wrote it would understand, or some gang sign. The kicker is the one that said, "I did your mom last night!" and so on and so forth.

Of course, that applied to bathroom walls too. They got their fair share of attention. Why hasn't anyone thought to paint the walls with chalkboard paint or wallpaper with poster board, provide markers and chalk and just let them go at it? Part of the fun is doing something they are not supposed to be doing, so it probably would stop if that were the case. Either way, it'd be a win-win for the store and the janitor who had to clean all that stuff up!

The Floral Department

People always seem to be smiling in the floral department. The employees are blessed to work in such a colorful, happy place in the market. They have flowers for every occasion; birthdays, weddings, graduation, and yes funerals, albeit a not-so-happy time. The creativity that comes from the floral department was only matched by Carrie's cakes from the bakery. Rosemary, who ran the floral department, took great pride in her flowers. Her name was appropriate too!

She had the domestic floral varieties, imported flowers, but most importantly, exotics! You know the ones; birds-of-paradise from Hawaii, orchids grown locally, and beautiful potted plants and arrangements in the cooler that she designed. Rosemary loved her job except for one day out of the year, Mother's Day. All holidays could be a challenge. Valentine's Day was a close second, but there's something about Mother's Day that was just out of control. Maybe it's because no one ever checked their calendar around the end of April or maybe because May 1st is May Day which was already a "flower-day" in the month of May. You know the one, where you are supposed to make a little basket full of flowers and put it on someone's doorknob, knock, and then run and hide?

May Day has its roots in the pagan, pre-Christian era when the Roman's worshiped Flora, the Goddess of flowers. The Druids in the British Isles celebrated May 1st as the Festival of Beltane which divided the year up in half. The other half of the year was known as Samhain, November 1, when fires were lit and the cattle were driven through it to purify them. It was a spring festival with a Maypole wrapped in colorful ribbons, singing, dancing, and cake. However, that's not commonly known or celebrated now in the U.S. These days May Day is a day for protesting everything from immigration, to labor inequities of the working class, to various social issues. Let's bring back the flowers and the singing, dancing, and cake!

Anyway, Rosemary always ran out of flowers on Mother's Day! All of those last minute shoppers who didn't get their mom's anything always resorted to flowers. So, even though she'd tripled her rose order, and her mums order, and her Lilly order, she just never had enough on hand to match the demand of the occasion! She didn't have enough space to order the amount she would need anyway, and she would never sell anyone a brown, or wilted flower! NEVER! Rosemary prided herself on her perfectionism. She always did quality work. Rosemary had worked at the market for 15 years and was known throughout the town as the best flower shop in the entire city. She was very proud of her reputation.

On one particular Mother's Day, she looked up from her work right into the eyes of a very handsome young man who had come into the market at 6:30 p.m. She was just about ready to close and go home because she had been working since 5:00 a.m. and was very tired. She let all her extra help go home and she was there alone wrapping things up.

The young man asked, "Excuse me, do you happen to have any flowers left? I've been to three other stores and nobody has anything."

Rosemary had already turned about a half-dozen people away. She felt heart-broken looking at this handsome young man who looked just as heart-broken. "I'm sorry," she said. "I just don't have anything left. I wish I did, but it's all gone."

She saw his eyes sink; his heart sank for him like no other customer she had given bad news to.

He said, "Oh, it's my fault. I waited too long. I've just been so busy with college and my job...my Mom deserves 1,000 boxes of roses! She works two jobs right now to help me with college and I couldn't even get here soon enough to get her favorite yellow roses."

A light went on in Rosemary's head. She remembered that earlier that day she took some yellow roses over to Cathy in the bakery to use on a cake. Maybe she hadn't used them all! She told the young man to wait and she would be right back. She walked over to the bakery and everyone was gone. She went straight to the cooler, and there in a jar were two perfect yellow roses! Hallelujah! Bingo!! Rosemary ran back to the floral department holding the roses behind her back. When she approached him, she brought out two of the most gorgeous, long-stemmed yellow roses the young man had ever seen. For a moment, his breath seemed to stop, but then a huge smile came across his face and he just lit up!

"You are an angel!" he beamed with joy.

That is why people work in customer service jobs. It's for all those days when the complainers are gone and moments like that when two simple yellow roses would be remembered for a lifetime. It's for that customer that knew quality when they saw it and were grateful to buy it. We all work hard for our money and we have a right to expect the best. Like the saying goes, the best money can buy.

The Deli

The larger stores struggle to give good customer service and the smaller stores are becoming obsolete, but that's usually where you will find the happiest people and the higher quality products. Employees of the smaller stores feel more like a family than like they are working for a company. It's a more supportive environment, more loving and more caring.

The deli girls started their day at 6:00 a.m. and made all the food for the day. Meat of all types were sliced and artfully arranged in the display case alongside about 15 different types of cheeses. It was an ongoing battle to keep the meat and cheese trays full and still keep them fresh. Cindy had just sliced and stocked the meat tray when a patron stepped up to the counter and asked, "Is this fresh?" Cindy wanted to yell, *doesn't it look fresh? What do you think lady? I'm standing here cleaning off the meat slicer!* Instead, she politely answered, "Yes ma'am, it's fresh. I just sliced it 10 minutes ago." Customer service was key!

That wasn't good enough for this customer. She wanted to see Cindy slice it right in front of her, which was her right. It was her money she had come to spend and she would get what she wanted!

Cindy smiled through her teeth and asked, "What would you like?"

The customer replied, "Half-pound of shaved, boiled ham, please."

That was the cheapest meat in the case, of course. Shaved meat was very, very thin and you got more for your dollar, but if the blade on your slicer was dull, you almost always needed to sharpen it, clean it, and then cut, all for $2.99 a pound. That was exactly what Cindy had to do. She asked the customer, "Do you have any more shopping to do?"

"No, I don't. I'll wait." She said.

"Ok, well, it will be a few minutes then. I'll do it as quickly as I can." Cindy replied.

The customer fidgeted and sounded impatient. "Well, hurry up. I haven't got all day!"

Cindy was not aware of her own body language and facial expressions. She really was trying to fulfill her customer's needs and finally concluded that she must just be having a bad day. She ran to the back room to get the boiled ham. She'd left the sharpener on hoping that by the time she got back it would be ready to go. By the time she ran back up to the deli counter, the customer had written a complaint about Cindy. Cindy thought *what have I done?* She tried to shrug it off, but she took everything to heart and was overly sensitive. She went back to the cooler, crying just a little because she had tried so hard to do everything right. Maybe a little too hard.

Cindy continued her shift, rearranging the salads in the salad case. She liked doing it because she enjoyed making it look fun and interesting. She used different colored bowls that always enhanced the color of the salads. She put bright green broccoli salad in the big blue bowl and the potato salad in the big red bowl. For her, it was artistic expression, a way to express her feelings. Sometimes she would wrap green onions around the edges of the potato salad so that it looked like a straw hat with a wispy brim. She loved doing the salad case.

When she was through with the cases, she took her first break of the day. The first break was supposed to be four hours after beginning of shift, but she didn't care. She didn't smoke like Laura did, and she didn't want to sit down because that would just make her remember how tired she was.

Sometimes, she would just go to the bathroom or go around to say hi to a few people in other departments, or she would take a walk outside to see what the weather was like. Fresh air was always good. She preferred being outside to staying inside all day anyway.

The hot case in the deli was handled by Laura. She was in the back cooking the fried and baked chicken; she'd get the breakfast burritos out first just in case anyone came in starving for breakfast. It was a standard hot case; chicken, macaroni and cheese, kielbasa on a stick, etc. Every day was the same except for one new entree. There was soup to defrost and heat up and it was always a race between Cindy and Laura to see who would get their case finished first. They made it fun!

Cindy and Laura respected each other, but deep down they didn't really like each other that much. Cindy thought Laura was a bitch and Laura thought everyone wasted too much time. The general consensus among staff was that they were both a lot alike. They were both hard working women and perfectionists. However, Cindy wasn't as rough around the edges as Laura was.

The mid-day shift was a somewhat productive shift. Sandwiches were made, dips on display, plenty of salads were made, and everything that was out in the self-same deli had to be stocked each night. The closing shift handled the hot case, filling it up throughout the night and then closed it down and finally cleaned it out. Each shift had its own personality and its own mood, if you will. On really busy days, the deli had a caterer. This meant work as usual with the same amount of duties and chores, but instead, 100 deviled eggs needed to be made plus two veggie trays and two fruit trays as well as one six-foot sub. There were small and large caterers and again, Cindy loved to make everything look good. She picked the freshest fruit, the firmest vegetables, and took a lot of satisfaction in going out on a catering job and setting the food up that she helped to prepare.

She loved to hear, *doesn't that look great? Boy, does this look good!* Everyone loves to hear positive comments. When the events were over, if there was any food left, some of the customers would take some home. Cindy would take what was left over if the client offered. She hated to see good food wasted.

One day, on a 6:00 a.m. shift that began at 4:00 a.m., Cindy and Laura had one of their best bonding experiences. They had to make nine, count them - NINE, 6-foot long sub-sandwiches. The bread was made in the bakery. It was twisted bread that had to be sliced right down the middle and then the fun began. Just like any good-ole' assembly line, the layers started first with the "special" spread that consisted of mayo and horseradish mustard. Then, the lettuce, tomatoes, pickles, onions and alternating meat and cheese; turkey, provolone, ham, Swiss, roast beef, and cheddar. To top it off, some big, black olives, about 50 of them were staked on toothpicks across the top.

The sandwiches were carefully wrapped up with bows on them, placed on boards to make it easier to be delivered and easier for customers to pick them up. There was supposed to be a $25 deposit for the boards because they never got the boards back. On that particular day, when Laura and Cindy met early to do the nasty deed with the help of Barb, all the meat had been sliced the day before, the tomatoes, onions, and everything else was ready to go, but they couldn't find any boards.

"What? No boards? How can this be?" exclaimed Cindy.

Matt was over in the meat department and had an idea. He had just gotten a wooden crate full of frozen hams and if he took the hams and put them in a cart to take back to the cooler, maybe he would be able to get some boards that Jerry had rigged up for the deli. It was truly a team effort. So, he set out to help in any way he could. The six-foot sub sandwiches ended up needing to be cut into 3-foot subs because Matt could only get 3-foot boards. It was the best they could do. Cindy, Laura, and Matt from the deli made it happen as a team. They felt good about improvising and making their large order a success.

Another bonding experience came one morning when Cindy was rushing to get the salad case filled and make it beautiful. She noticed the light bulb in her case was out and there were only six very long lights in her case, instead of seven and it was looking a little dark in there. Unfortunately, it happened right after Cindy had just finished putting in her last salad bowl. She wondered if she should leave the burnt out light in the case or try to maneuver it out from its place. Being the perfectionist that she was, she decided simply to get it out of there. As gracefully as she could, she reached back in and tried to pull out the 7-foot long fluorescent light when, just then, a customer came up to the counter asking for help.

Cindy raised up her head to say hello and in that split second everything went to Hell. Imagine you are about to fall and you think, *oh God, I'm going down,* or like the second you look down to change the CD in your car while you are driving and you look up to see you have swerved into the opposite lane. You suddenly realize you are on a head-on collision course with oncoming traffic and you over-correct the wheel only to fish-tail down the road before gaining control of your vehicle again, heart thumping wildly. Cindy had that split-second feeling and immediately the light bulb broke into a million tiny glass shards all over the salads that she had just finished neatly placing in the case!

Dear God, this can't be happening right now! Cindy thought to herself, trying to keep her composure in front of the customer. Like most days, Laura had finished setting up her case ahead of Cindy and was outside puffing on her cigarette and sipping her coffee. She had no idea that everything was ruined.

Cindy turned to the customer and said, "What may I get you? She sounded very distraught.

"Well, certainly not any of those salads with the glass in them!" She replied astonished at what had just happened.

Cindy thought *what a compassionate person you are!* Once again, her day was not starting out well.

"There are some salads that didn't get the shards of glass in them or there is a salad bar right behind you that Laura just got through setting up. You are welcome to help yourself." Cindy tried to keep her composure but felt the blood rush to her face.

"I never eat off salad bars. There are just too many germs!" The customer exclaimed. "What is your name? Oh, Cindy, I see your name tag. Well, good luck with the rest of your day. You just lost a customer!" She walked away.

Cindy felt like crying. Not only were all of the salads ruined, but she just couldn't take another customer complaint that day! She thought *I can't take this. I get up every morning and make dinner for my sons because I know that when I get off work I'll be too tired to make dinner for them. I go to work and do my best and all I get is complaints, and stress! I give up!* Cindy was seriously contemplating walking off the job.

Who would pay the high mortgage if she did that? Who would pay her son's dental bills, and for her son's new baseball mitt and her other son's soccer shoes? She could already hardly live on her very small child support and the wages she earned. There was a time when she was working two jobs; 6:00 a.m. to 2:00 p.m. at the market and 3:00 p.m. to 11:00 p.m. at the factory making a popular nose spray. It became physically impossible so she had to scale back. She kept her job at the market to be with her kids after school and in the evenings. Her kids meant the world to her and she would never jeopardize the ability to care for them or spend time with them.

Laura rounded the corner to see Cindy literally falling apart and asked, "What happened?" Even though they were constantly trying to out-do the other, Laura saw a disaster as her time to really shine. She grabbed a Kleenex for Cindy and told her to go in the back room and start throwing some cole slaw together. That seemed like an easy enough task since it came into the deli already shredded and all they had to do was add the dressing.

"Get out of here and go in the back! I'll get these salads out of here as fast as I can and dump the ones that have glass in them. I just pray the ones I leave don't have any!" She exclaimed.

Cindy, through her tears, was thanking Laura knowing deep down that they had a bond that would never be replaced by anyone. Cindy headed to the back kitchen to make more salads. Laura had gotten a cart to throw all the salads on and was filling the cart when the PIC walked back to the deli asking to talk with Cindy.

"There's been another complaint," the PIC said.

"Ben, I've been here the whole time and Cindy had an accident, an unforeseeable accident in the salad case. Although I was not out front, I was in the back," Laura lied. She had actually been on her smoke break.

"I heard the whole conversation and Cindy was not rude, she even offered to help in the middle of the catastrophe and the woman wouldn't hear anything of the sort!" Laura flat-out lied to protect Cindy.

Maybe Laura did have a heart and maybe all her toughness and competitiveness just developed over the years but it appeared that Cindy had an ally that she wasn't even aware of. Or maybe, just maybe, Laura really wanted to get that salad case filled back up because the lunch crowd would be coming in soon and there was going to be an even bigger mess in that deli if things weren't ready for the rush.

It didn't matter to Cindy what the reason was for Laura's lie, she was just so thankful to not have to be out in front. She felt better being in the back kitchen making salads as fast as she could. She didn't have the energy to paste on a smile; she just put her head down and was focused on the tasks at hand. She could be real with herself then, not fake and disingenuous.

Customer service is where you will find the best actors and actresses; day after day. Rain or shine no matter what has happened to you at home, at work, or in your personal life. You have to put on your "happy face" and radiate a desire to serve your fellow man/woman like a Private serves a General, like a dog serves a master. It can be very rewarding, or it can be very painful, but it is one's job to serve and, hey, if you don't like it, quit.

Well, Cindy and Laura share another very strong trait; they aren't quitters. Within 25-30 minutes, the case was free of all glass and four new salads Cindy had made in record time. A miracle!! No, a team effort actually. Cindy looked at Laura and said one word, "thanks." Laura looked at her and said one word, "welcome." The day continued as if nothing happened.

The Meat Department

The deli and the meat department were right next to each other. Fran, from the deli, occasionally rotated over to help Matt or Mandy, the full-time meat wrappers, on their days off. She also helped Matt on holidays such as Christmas and Thanksgiving when there were tons of turkeys, hams, roasts, etc. It was a nightmare, but a lot of money was made during those blessed events and everybody knew the holiday dinner centered on the platter of poultry, pork, or beef!!

Matt asked that people place their special orders at least a week in advance so he didn't over or under-order for the holidays. It was an art and a science and nobody wanted to be stuck with 30 hams after the holidays, although if he ordered them fresh he could always stick them in his broken down freezers. Remember, he was supposed to be getting new ones!!

That particular year, he anticipated selling 200 turkey's, 300 prime ribs, and 300 hams for Christmas. He'd also thrown in a few crown roasts, those circles of lamb ribs with the white paper chef hats on top of each one. They look like a lot of little bakers holding hands at a bakery convention. He'd also get a few tenderloin roasts ordered and on occasion, a goose or duck. He had always wondered why people didn't eat more fish around the holidays but it's all about tradition in the United States. We don't really have a lot of traditions since we are such a hodge-podge of mixed mongrels, so depending on whether you have any Irish, Scottish, English, French, Indian, or other culture in your blood, we here in the good 'ole U.S.A. will never see lutefisk and lefse on our Christmas table unless you have a traditional Norwegian background, and even then most are so Americanized anyway.

Matt was very stressed out during the holidays but you would never know it. He always had the same constant smile and the same quiet disposition. He did his job well and was popular at the market. Everyone through the holidays kept asking him how he was doing because most people would be having a heart attack, but Matt seemed to be looking and acting the same as ever. Matt had a system of course, and expected the increase in activity. He had everything in alphabetical order on his clipboard; the name of the customer, what they had ordered, the size of the order, and any special instructions, as well as the initials of who took the order in case there was any question he would know who to go to for the answers. On that day, he parceled up the orders, wrapped and labeled them with their name and put them back in the meat department cooler awaiting that sacred pick-up.

It all went down like clockwork most of the time, but every holiday you could be sure that at least two or three monumental events happened, mix-ups if you will, that went down in the history books of moments they'd want to forget.

Take the year the Levin's, a Jewish family, ordered a beautiful prime rib roast, got it home, and unfolded the white paper only to find an un-blessed spiral ham! Or, the year the Wilkinson's ordered an organic turkey, because really they were vegetarians but once a year they ate organic turkey, spent twice as much money as anybody else just to get the organic one, and got it home, unwrapped the white paper only to find a natural turkey. That meant it didn't have any of the injected butters, etc. but, it wasn't organic. They cooked it up anyway and then got sick and ended up blaming the meat department exclusively for making them all ill.

Three days later, Mrs. Wilkinson discovered it wasn't the turkey after all, it was the deviled eggs that Aunt Sue had left out all night on her counter because her refrigerator was too packed full to put them in. She thought they would be alright because, well by golly, the eggs had been cooked! The Wilkinson's actually had taken their turkey to the health department and every possible test had shown no bacteria, or any other reason for the blame to fall on the turkey, natural, as it was. So Matt was off the hook.

The biggest mess always seemed to be from the husbands who came in to pick up the order their wives had carefully placed with the date and time, but the order was nowhere to be found. This happened to Matt over and over again. The answer was always the same because Matt's system had never failed him. Well, maybe once or twice, because nothing was foolproof. The answer was simply that they went to the wrong market! Yep, that's right!! Communication, communication, communication!

It's a little known fact that most husbands and wives, after the first 2-5 years really stop talking to each other or listening, so during the holidays it becomes even more true. Time after time, you would see an angry customer back in the meat department demanding his or her parcels when in fact, it was at another store and they didn't have a parcel at this one because an order was actually never placed.

It was a very stressful time and if someone came in asking for their order, Matt had to check his inventory at least three times, call to have another person come in because, by golly, Matt was only human and he may not see it amongst the hundreds of special orders. He double-checked his clipboard clockwise and counterclockwise just to be sure. Then, he'd gently ask the customer, "are you sure your wife [husband] placed an order with us?"

Now, cellphones are a wonderful thing and if the customer didn't have one, well Matt would definitely offer up his meat department phone to anybody to make double sure that the order was with him. In fact, he would bend over backwards, so to speak, to calm anyone's stress at a time of such high anxiety. Hell, he'd gotten phone calls from other stores himself when the exact situation had happened at another store, and if nothing could be found, believe me, he would make sure no one went home without their main course!

Bill Payne had come to the meat department to pick up his order. It was a 15-pound rib roast ordered by his wife a week prior. Matt couldn't find her name on his list and he even checked for different spellings, like P A I N, or any other way he can think of.

"What's her first name?" Matt asked.

"Dawn Payne." Bill said.

Matt thought that maybe someone put it down as "Don Payne," or "Don Pain," or something like that. Who knew? There was nothing even close to it on his list. The meat department could be a pretty loud place when the slicer was running. Matt saw the meat wrapping machine, so he looked really fast for a name like "Cane," or anything that could possibly be misunderstood over the phone, and asked for their home telephone number. He quickly went through the list of numbers to see if he could find a match, but came up with nothing. He went into the back cooler to look on the alphabetized cooler racks....P...P...P...where are the P's? No Payne. There was Palm, Pearson, Prather, but no Payne anywhere. Matt slowly turned and was getting prepared to ask Mr. Payne the dreaded question.

"Mr. Payne," Matt asked. "Could you please call your wife and ask again what day she ordered this roast and exactly from whom? I'm sure it's just a simple mistake."

Bill said the unthinkable. "She's flying in from out of town right now. I can't get a hold of her. This is crazy. I know she ordered it from you. It's a 15-pound prime rib. I don't believe this!" Bill was getting agitated.

Matt went into action. He went back into the cooler, grabbed his apron on his way and went to his back stock of beef, grabbed the quarter of beef, threw it on his saw and proceeded to cut Mr. Payne his prime rib with an additional 3 pounds for free. All the while, Mr. Payne was frantically on his cell phone, but he couldn't get through to his wife. Matt came out carrying the big white parcel.

"No worries, Mr. Payne. I just cut you a fresh 18 pounder, but I'll only charge you for 15. Have a great Thanksgiving or Christmas or whatever this holiday is." Matt said. Thanksgiving and Christmas seemed to run together for him.

Bill put away his phone and a smile came across his face. "Wow, three pounds of free meat! You sure took care of me, didn't you?" Bill thanked Matt and told him that he was in real estate and if he ever needed anything to give him a call and handed him his business card. Matt shook his hand and said thanks to Bill then headed back to the phone in the meat department. Just for a lark, he called to another store six blocks away, a bigger store than his market, and asked for the meat department. He was put on hold for a long while and when someone finally picked up the first thing they said was, "Meat department. Please hold." Don't you just hate that when you've been put on hold forever and then they finally pick up and put you on hold again?

Finally, someone came back on the line and Matt asked, "Do you have an order for Dawn or Bill Payne for prime rib?"

"Please hold," they say again. After about six or eight minutes, which felt like eternity, Matt heard what he wanted to hear.

"Yes, we do." Matt thanked him and chuckled, put down the receiver smiling and thought *I knew it! I just knew it! Wrong store!*

Matt took a week off work after the holidays. For the first two days he would dream of turkeys pecking him, cows jumping off his butcher block, and fun stuff like that. Then, he and his wife would take a day for them to go out to dinner where he would order salmon and she would order shrimp. Then he would spend the rest of the time with his family. Matt had two beautiful daughters who were very emotionally and physically healthy and he was very proud of them. They were a very stable family, no addictions, no major problems, which was very rare in American society or anywhere these days for that matter. The saying that they just don't make them like that anymore definitely applied to Matt and his family. It was an honor to work with someone like Matt at the market.

The Dairy Case

The dairy case got re-stocked daily and usually at least two to three times. You might ask why, it's just milk and what about all those other perishable items that need refrigeration and sell fast like; cheese, whip cream, yogurt, etc. There are rows and rows of product that need to be re-filled so that the consumer feels that there is great care taken on every shelf. All of the containers needed to be lined up perfectly with proper labels, no exceptions. If the stock was clear to the back so the customer wouldn't see it, or couldn't reach it, then most likely they wouldn't buy it, heaven forbid, so the dairy stock boys who checked rotation of product made sure the milk in front said June 2018 if it was June 2018, or whatever date it happened to be. A customer should never find a bottle of milk that said February 2018 because that could make someone very sick.

The dairy stockers also stocked the self-serve meats and cheese, the hot dogs, bologna, Swiss and cheddars, etc. They all had dates on them and if they were not sold by their expiration they got pulled from the shelf. It was a big chore to keep up on it and was only given to the most responsible front end courtesy clerks. They scrambled to the back of the store to do their duty whenever there was some down time; basically when nobody was there, no customers, that is. One courtesy clerk would stay up front, but if they did, and there were no customers, their responsibility was to take an aisle and go down it pulling everything forward to keep the store looking nice and well-stocked throughout the day. They didn't want there to be any holes, all products must be to the front and facing forward like little soldiers at attention just waiting for the arrival of the hand that would pluck them down and throw them into the shopping cart or basket.

Jason was back "working" the dairy case on one Tuesday afternoon when a group of long-haired Gypsies came into the store; two girls and two guys. They were dressed in velvet and silks and smelled of lavender. They were laughing their heads off about some beaded necklace that had gotten caught in one of the guy's long, red hair. Jason looked right when he was filling the milk shelf. His hand reached out and back very fast trying to be as efficient as he could as one Gypsy girl spoke of chocolate milk.

"I need chocolate milk," Jason heard her say. Jason was just starting to fill the chocolate milk one motion after another like a machine. His arm grabbed the product from its plastic crate and placed it on the shelf filling it as fast as he could go. The girl reached in to get some chocolate milk at the exact moment that Jason was reaching in with the container from the back of the cooler. The girl screamed as she saw an arm hand her a container of chocolate milk!

"Oh my God!! I just saw an arm in the cooler!! Oh my God, oh my God!!" She was laughing hysterically because she couldn't see anybody in there, only an arm and a hand.

The others gathered around to try and see what she saw as she was laughing hysterically. What they saw was a human arm moving faster than the speed of light filling, filling, filling the dairy case up with milk. Of course Jason was the culprit, the man behind the "arm" but they couldn't see his body. The girl was soon on the floor in the middle of the aisle laughing uncontrollably.

"I can't stop laughing...I peed my pants! Oh my God!!" She sputtered through her tears of hysteria.

Her friends started laughing with her and it became quite a sight to see in the dairy aisle. She put down the milk and ran from the store. Maybe it was from embarrassment, after all, she did pee her bright orange velvet pants, or maybe it was paranoia? Who knows, but they all followed her out of the store without purchasing anything. Jason wondered what they were on. It must've been some good stuff. He had never seen anyone so happy or crazy over chocolate milk before!

Two weeks later, Jason was in the front end of the store when an old school bus pulled up and out crawled thirteen very young kids ages 15-21. They were dressed all in black with big black, dark eyes, big, chunky black boots, chains, tattoos, and piercings everywhere! It was like a Gothic circus caravan! Most of them had all black leather on, some of the girls wore black lace, but everything was black. A very mournful looking group; even their dogs had big, black leather collars with spikes coming out of them. There were three dogs and looked like pit-bull mixes with lots of scars. One of the girls was visibly pregnant.

The whole store shook with fear when they saw them coming in the front door of the store. The door parted and in they came like a pack of wild dogs hooting and hollering and getting in the electric wheelchair and racing carts all over the store. Of course, the old security guard was a no-show that particular day so the PIC who just, by luck of the draw, happened to be skinny Greg, was the person watching out. He couldn't believe what he was about to be faced with.

They started filling up the carts with chips, cereal and candy...oh and SpaghettiOs! It's likely they ate them right out of the can! They eventually had three full carts with everything including dog food, candles, you name it. Everyone was completely sure they were going to make a mad dash for the front door. Greg went up and asked them, as politely as he could, to take their dog out of the store. There were no dogs allowed, *not even human dogs*, Greg thought as he got closer and closer to the really bad smell. It was just patchouli oil, but as the shopping spree continued, the young pregnant girl went back to the deli. She needed some protein and she needed it right away. She wasn't feeling very well and she went up to the hot case to see Laura putting the fresh baked chicken inside.

"Boy that smells good!" She said. Laura grunted at her and turned away.

Cindy came up and asked, "Hi, is there anything I can get you?"

The girl was so hungry. She wanted it all. She looked at Cindy and said, "Sure. I'd like eight chicken legs and four breasts."

Cindy looked down at her round frame thinking *she's so young. Maybe 16-17 years old. What kind of life was this child going to have?*

Cindy said, "My name is Cindy. What's yours?"

"Ren," she replied.

"Ren, that's a pretty name. I've never heard that name before." Cindy smiled at the girl.

"It was my mother's name," the girl said as she broke down in tears. "She and dad were killed in a car accident last year. They were going to make me go live with my grandmother who hates me so I ran away."

Cindy could not believe her ears and then, of course, it all made sense. These were all lost kids. She was expecting to see Peter Pan fly down any minute but what she got instead was the father of the child who walked up beside Ren, his name was Black. He was 18 and the captain of the bus.

Black peered into the hot case and said, "Hun, are you about ready to go? Did you get you and the baby some protein?"

"Yes," she said. "I was just having a conversation with this nice lady, Cindy. This is my partner, Black." Black reached out his gloved hand and shook Cindy's. *What nice respectful young people,* Cindy thought.

Ren turned and said, "I know we are young, but we are in love and I haven't any family other than our 'group'. Black and I decided we needed to make more of our own family. He doesn't have a family either but he was left a lot of money and he's taking care of all of us."

Cindy turned to Black and asked him where they were staying.

"In our bus," he answered.

"I have a big house about four blocks from here. Would you like to come and at least sleep on the floor, all of you?" Cindy asked.

Black looked deep into Cindy's eyes and said, "That would be so great but we need to be somewhere by the morning. But thanks for the offer. Really! It's really nice of you!"

They all said their good-byes. Cindy turned to Ren and said, "Drink lots of water, keep eating protein, get your rest, etc." Ren promised that she would.

They went up to the check stand, paid for all their groceries and Black went over to the floral department and bought a single red rose and gave it to the PIC up front. He said, "Would you make sure you give this to Cindy? Tell her I will never forget her kindness."

Greg walked back to the deli with the most beautiful red rose. He handed it to Cindy, which took her aback because she knew Greg liked her as a friend but this was too much! Open affection right there in the middle of the deli?

Greg smiled and said, "No, it's not from me. It's from the leader of the pack. You know, that group dressed in black?"

Cindy said, "Yea, weren't they interesting?"

"I don't know, I was pretty scared." Greg said. Cindy turned to Greg after she had heard those words and asked, "Hey, do you know what all the colors of the rainbow mixed together make?"

Greg said he didn't know. "Black" said Cindy. Greg nodded his head, turned and walked away. Black. Never judge a book by its cover.

Left Behind

Three weeks later another bus pulled up at the market. This time it was a larger tour bus from Vancouver, B.C. with 40 or 50 Japanese tourists on it. None of them spoke English. The call went out through the store to locate anyone who spoke Japanese. Carrie had an adopted daughter from Japan, but that really didn't help because ever since Jade was six months old, she'd been living with Carrie. She didn't know much about Jade's parents either. She did know one word in Japanese though. An informal greeting, Ohayō! So, she told everyone to just say "Ohayō!" and that's about all she could do to help. Everyone in the store was saying "Ohayō" to the tourists.

They descended upon the bakery, the deli, and the coffee stand. It was amazing to see how people communicated yet didn't speak the same language. They all seemed to get what they wanted and were very happy. After loading back onto the bus and driving off, one of the young girls came out of the bathroom. They had left her behind! She walked to the window and pointed down the road at the back of the bus driving off. It was clear by the expression on her face that she couldn't believe they had left without her. What was she going to do?

She started to cry and everyone at the front of the store surrounded her which made her seem even more nervous. She began to speak very fast in Japanese and once again, confusion and mayhem ensued at the market. Mandy from the coffee stand came over and told them to leave the poor girl alone, that they were scaring her to death! She took the girl to the coffee stand for some Jasmine tea and called a friend who worked at the University to find out if there was anybody who spoke Japanese and could help. This idea sounded great to everyone in the store and they backed off and gave her some space. She was reluctant to leave the front of the store because she was sure they would notice she was missing and turn around and come back, but she went with Mandy and sat on a stool behind the counter, still speaking in Japanese and clearly wondering why they would just leave her there!

Mandy made Mocha for a customer and then the phone rang. She found out that there was a professor who had just returned from Japan and would be down in a few minutes to offer his assistance. Mandy kept smiling at the young girl and patting her shoulder which seemed to have a calming effect on her. The professor tried to tell her how to say he'd be there as fast as he can in Japanese, but Mandy told him to forget it. She only took a quarter of Spanish in school and she could rattle on in English but that was about it.

The professor showed up at the market after about an hour. So much for, "I'll be right there!" What, did he read three thesis papers before he left? Anyway, he walked into the store and headed straight for the coffee stand. Mandy had told him on the phone that he would find them there. When she saw him, she stood up and started talking a mile a minute and he was listening, trying to keep up with her. It turned out that he knew the young girl's father who was also a professor. They smiled and laughed and he took her to his home for dinner and a place to stay.

In the morning he would personally drive her back up to Vancouver, B.C. where she was attending college and everything would be peachy keen except that during this whole ordeal, she had discovered that her passport was still on the bus in her backpack!

Since the professor was very well-known, and had come very close to adopting the castaway for a day or two, he successfully got her across the border and back to school. For that, he received two cantaloupes in the mail wrapped in velvet, one of the most honorable gifts you could receive in Japanese culture, because believe it or not, cantaloupes in Japan could go for up to $250 each! Go figure!

The Mohawk Bandit

Across from the market there was a bank. To get to the front door, you had to go down a little hill. For some reason, that bank had been robbed eight times in the past two years. They had real security cameras and during all of the robberies, there was a full-time security guard on duty at the front door, which was very expensive. The last robbery occurred in the middle of the day, around 4:00 p.m. People at the market wouldn't have known that except that the robber came into the store.

Some people who rob banks do so very carefully, keep a low profile, and are dressed plainly so as not to cause attention to themselves. However, this time that was not the case. The assailant had a Mohawk painted all different colors, his pants were nearly falling off his body and he had very bad body odor that alone, would turn your head and make you look, but your nose would turn right back around. He was anything but incognito as he came bounding through the side door by the coffee shop, ordered a coffee and went to the bakery to get a doughnut. That's right! He had just robbed a bank and was going to spend the first of his new-found dough on a donut and coffee!

While some would consider these actions a little bit risky, since everyone and their mother would be on the lookout for someone with his wild hairstyle that was exactly what he did. Rather than pay at the coffee stand and escape through the side door, he proceeded to go to the front check stand and wait in line for about five minutes. What happened next would baffle even the most experienced psychologist. The woman in front of him in line, with two small children, didn't have enough to pay for all of her groceries. The checker was asking her what she would like to put back. Out of nowhere, the guy with the rainbow Mohawk pulled out his wad of cash and paid for everything! She was stunned! Shocked! Everyone in line was astounded at his generosity.

The woman wanted to get his address to be able to send him the money and pay him back for his kindness. He insisted it wasn't necessary. Of course it wasn't necessary! It wasn't even his money. Mr. Henry's recent deposit at the bank just bought her groceries! He was trying to get out of the store when he saw the police coming in the same side door he had just nonchalantly walked through only 15-20 minutes before. He threw down a $20 bill for his coffee and donut and said he had to go. Out he flew! The woman commented on how nice a young man he was even though he did smell pretty bad. As the police were walking very briskly up and down the aisles looking for "rainbow Mohawk man" (they dubbed him), Rainbow was jumping onto the bus out in front of the store.

Ben, the lead checker, had turned just in time to see him get onto the bus. The police came up to the check stands. One was very heavy set with a mustache. He was in charge of dragging three more cops behind him and spoke first.

"We are looking for a young man around 5' 11" with a Mohawk with all sorts of colors in it. Have you seen him?" The police officer asked.

Ben looked around at the other checkers. He couldn't possibly mean that nice young, generous, smelly Robin Hood! Ben looked at the police. The policemen looked at Ben, eyebrows raised. Ben looked at the lady with her kids and said very quietly, "he just got on that bus."

The police ran outside to their patrol cars and radioed the bus terminal. The head dispatcher called the bus driver to inquire and sure enough Rainbow was sitting right there in the front seat.

"Oh my God." The bus driver wondered instantly if he was packing a piece and wondering what he should do now.

Luckily, his route took him within 50 feet of the police station and he was ordered to drive the bus to the police station and let him off there. Then, they called back and said that he should just stick to his normal route and they would grab him when he got off the bus. If he had pulled up to the police station who knew what the young man would do. He may have taken hostages, started shooting, or who knows what.

So, the bus driver stuck to his normal route and pulled up at the bookstore right across from the station, let the boy out, and within the time it takes you to slap a mosquito off your arm, he was in handcuffs!

Back at the store, the news had spread like wildfire with many different versions, thanks to Mandy. There was one version where he had a knife or switch-blade and one where he had a gun and one where he wasn't armed at all. Someone even said he had taken a hostage from the store onto the bus when the police showed up. Another rumor was that the girl in front of him with the two kids was his girlfriend and it was all some sort of scam! It was incredible!

The fact remained that from the time he had robbed the bank at 4:00 pm and went into the store, paid for one lucky customers grocery bill of $75.84, got his coffee and donut, and boarded the bus only to get caught 8 miles away, only 45 minutes had gone by. A robbery and capture within 45 minutes! The police force was pretty proud of themselves, but really, who robs a bank and then goes and buys coffee and donuts? Especially someone as obvious as he was with a rainbow Mohawk on a Friday night. Ironically, it was Friday the 13th!

Grievances

The market was full of challenges; high points, low points, and everything in between. A good day was when all employees showed up when they were supposed to and the department heads could get their work done, complete their production lists, have lunch, and go home on time. This particular market was in the Local 44 Retail Clerks union and all managers were paid a salary, everyone else was paid hourly wages. The store owners generally got along with the union, or at least tolerate them, but they didn't like the fact that they had to pay the employees a wage set down by the union rather than the state.

People were being hired at minimum wage and then those with six years seniority were getting paid $11.50 per hour according to their union contract and what they had determined to be valuable time spent in perfecting their trade. Those folks were called "journeymen". You also had the apprentices and the Senior Journeyman rates. The Journeymen and Senior Journeymen got medical, dental, guaranteed lunch breaks, and other benefits. The employer must also pay the union dues every month which were deducted from employee's paychecks. If they fell behind more than three months, they could lose their job and were not in good standing anymore with the union.

Laura, from the Deli, was good friends with the union representative

71

for the store. They went way back and Laura was the eyes and ears of the union. When any problems arose, she was on the phone in a heartbeat, which really didn't do much good because you could report a whole lot of stuff to the union and it would take them months before they would do anything about it anyway.

There was a schedule posted in the deli that had to be completed by 5:00 pm every Friday for the following week. On this particular Friday, there was no schedule on the wall. Everybody was calling in to get their schedule and Laura was pissed off because she was tired of answering the phone. She knew that if she were running that deli, the schedule would be up and in place every week.

She called the deli manager at home, but he was nowhere to be found. He must've been out eating dinner with his wife or something, so she grabbed a blank schedule and started filling it out herself. She took the schedule from the week before and pretty much just copied it. She didn't know that Cindy had asked for a particular day off for a doctor's appointment and, more importantly, for her son's birthday and she also didn't realize that Barb needed a day for her dentist appointment. She had gotten her braces in a never-ending battle to make herself feel better about herself, and Mandy, who had three days more seniority for this one time had her name below Laura's. It usually read according to seniority; Mandy, Laura, Barb, then Cindy.

Mandy went back into the deli to write down her schedule and was mortified to see Laura's name above hers. So, she immediately called the union! Cindy called the union because she hadn't asked for a day off in six months and she didn't get her requested day off. The union was wondering what the heck was going on there and it appeared sheer mutiny would happen if somebody didn't do something about this fiasco.

The store owner was off golfing when the union called, so he asked for the PIC on duty. It was Sam's unfortunate luck to have to take the call and he explained that he didn't know what was going on in the deli. The union rep told Sam they had gotten at least four phone calls already that day and that he needed to go over there and put up a sign. The sign should read, "Schedule will be posted on Monday. Sorry for the inconvenience." Sam was also told to take down the schedule that was up there because they didn't want to get anymore phone calls about it and furthermore they didn't care how much money people were paying in dues, the phone calls needed to STOP!

Rumor had it that the store manager could be fired by the union if the schedules were not posted on time and everyone knew the deli would be at fault. Sam trotted on back to the deli and said hello to Laura. He told her he'd just received a phone call from the union complaining about the schedules and all of the phone calls they had been receiving left and right.

"I have to nip this in the butt!" Sam said.

Laura stood there dumbfounded because she had only tried to help. "This is the last straw! I am sick and tired of covering for the Deli Manager! This store is run very poorly and the owner has no clue what he is doing. He's out of his freaking mind!"

It was the end of Laura's shift anyway so when he saw her get her jacket and get ready to leave, Sam thought, she'll be back. However, Laura didn't come back for a full three weeks! They called it a leave of absence, they called it a "Laura vacation," but really she just needed time to calm herself down.

While Laura was away, the deli was more calm and organized than ever. It took a lot of work from everyone, but they were suddenly stress-free, relaxed, and happy. By the time she went back to work, she didn't speak to anybody for the first full week, unless it was business and absolutely necessary. There were no dirty jokes and no butt-squeezing. She was certainly not herself. Slowly, as time went on, she got over it and life resumed as normal once again, or at least semi-normal. After all, what was normal for life at the market?

Ed

Speaking of not being normal, Ed was far from normal! Ed had been shopping at the market for about three years. He always had something wrong with him and every week it was something new. First, they found out that he had Diabetes. The next week, it was an ear infection. Conversations with Ed were always around his health and diet, his lack of exercise, etc. Nobody in the market wanted to ask him the usual greeting, "How are you today Mr. Hall?" They knew that would mean a 20-30 minute update on his health conditions and every illness known to man! Mandy, in the coffee shop, actually gave up trying to help him and if she had given up, rest assured, there was no hope.

Ed headed back to the produce department because someone had told him that if he ate peppers, it would bring his blood pressure down. Jason was there trimming the lettuce to make the display look prettier when Ed started to reach for a red pepper near the lettuce. All of a sudden, Ed grabbed Jason's arm as he was falling to the ground! Ed's face began to turn purple. Jason grabbed Ed and hoisted him back up and with one swift Heimlich-like maneuver that propelled the gum right out of Ed's throat. Ed and Jason collapsed down to the floor. They were both breathing heavily! The color slowly normalized in Ed's face and he put his hand over his heart, grateful he didn't choke.

Right at that moment, in walked the most beautiful, long-legged, raven-haired woman either man had ever seen. She had the shortest white skirt on that with a little red ruffle and a tank top with no bra. She seemed to be cooled in the air-conditioned store because her nipples were about as erect as they could get except when feeding a newborn baby! She was walking right over to where the two men were sitting on the floor, catching their breath from the near-choking incident. She leaned over between them to get a red pepper and the men discreetly noticed she was not wearing any panties! Oh my, the men were speechless! In fact they stopped breathing for a minute until she looked down at them.

"Hi guys, just getting a red pepper. What are you doing on the floor?" she asked.

Neither one could find their voice. They didn't say a word. They averted their eyes and waited in silence until she walked away so they could regain their composure.

Jason looked at Ed and said, "Well, that was all worth it!"

Ed replied, "Yep, if I die tomorrow I'll go a happy man."

They both laughed and stood up and went about their day. From then on, whenever Jason and Ed saw each other in the produce section of the store, Jason would ask how he's feeling. Ed would pick-up a red pepper and say, "Fine, just fine. I'm just getting a red pepper!" From that day forward he ate a lot more red peppers than he ever had and actually his health was improving. He didn't complain near as much as he had before.

Sometimes we all need to complain a little. It's the human way to cleanse or purge, if you will. When we are sad, when we are in pain, there are times when we are looking for comfort. There are times when we are calling out to our fellow man, or woman, for compassion and hope to find the strength to go on even when things aren't so great. Some people are born complainers and others develop it over the years from their upbringing and life experiences. We often don't know what is behind one's suffering, but certainly lending an ear costs us nothing. If you take time to listen to someone in need, hopefully when you need someone to lend an ear, someone will be there. Karma.

The Red Baron

Sales representatives that came into the store were an interesting breed of folks. They were usually very good looking, out-going, and bubbly, had good teeth, and were very well-dressed. Of course they wanted to give a good impression so that you would buy what they are selling and put it in your store. They would talk to you for hours, even take you to lunch, leave samples, and do whatever they needed to do to make a sale. Sometimes they would even do a special promotion by giving away prizes to entice you to use their products! These displays were usually very big and got in the way. Most employees couldn't wait for them to be removed.

Take, for instance, when a local beer factory wanted to bring a big, stuffed (as in taxidermy) beaver into the store and put it on the front end aisle facing the checkout stands. The owner flat out said no. Then there was the trail mix company that wanted to bring in a real life-sized canoe full of mannequins with backpacks and suspend it from the ceiling. The owner, again, said no. It was too risky. What if it fell on a customer? Talk about a lawsuit waiting to happen!

However, when this very pretty representative wanted to put up a display of four kites in the store to promote her kite business, the owner agreed. After all, everyone loves kites. It's a fun activity anyone can to with their kids, a boyfriend/girlfriend, their parents, basically it's fun for all! So, she was invited back to hang the kites for display. She hung them close to the check stands so everyone could see them. There was a rainbow boat kite, a dragon kite, a pirate ship kite, and one red kite shaped like a plane. It was just like the one Snoopy flew as the Red Baron. Well, all Hell broke loose over that one!

The owner started getting letters from Jewish people asking if he knew what he was displaying in his store! German folks didn't like it either saying that the blood-red plane represented evil and death or that it stood for Hitler. The owner heard so much controversy over the red plane kite that he wondered why in the world, just because something was displayed in the store that it meant it symbolized one's own personal beliefs. It was ridiculous and the owner was pissed off. The sign on his desk never rang more true. It read, "The quickest way to failure is to try to please everyone." However, isn't that what customer service is all about? Pleasing everyone or, at least trying to?

The owner held his ground. He put a small stuffed bear in the cockpit of the red plane kite, complete with a leather jacket, goggles and a flying cap on its head which slightly softened the impact of the plane for about a week. It became the talk of the store about whether it should stay or go. The containers of kites for sale represented by the ones hung from the ceiling were still full by the end of the week except for one. The one with the red baron kite! People are funny. The owner snickered when he heard that. No, he wasn't a Communist, a Socialist, or trying to make a political statement of any kind. He was just a businessman trying to make a living knowing that try as you may, you cannot please everybody.

Occupational Hazards

In every workplace, there are occupational hazards. Forget the mental turmoil, there's counseling for that, but the market had their fair share of physical injuries. Remember the greenhorn cutting across his thigh with his knife? It's time to get a little more specific and this is not for the weak hearted.

Let us begin with the checkout stands.

Occupational hazard number one: standing in one place all day on a little 12 inch rubber mat. When it comes to the twisting over and over again, dragging products across the laser, reaching, pulling, and lifting, while the right hand is on the register punching in numbers and looking up codes, there are hazards everywhere. Some will wear those black Velcro support belts underneath their uniform so as not to look like they are injured. The repetitive motions and constant standing can affect your back, your wrists, your neck, your feet, and just about every part of your body.

Occupational hazard number two: continuous, repetitive motions can lead to carpal tunnel syndrome. Often, the checkers would wear wrist braces to try and protect their wrists. Many had to have surgery, and some were just trying to avoid it altogether. The pain of this affliction is immense and has led to needing to leave work early, miss work, or move more slowly reducing productivity. It can cause one to wake in the middle of the night to have a drink, or take a pain killer because your arm is just aching and your fingers are numb from the pain.

Checkers do fairly well financially, usually making anywhere from $15 - 18 dollars an hour but is any amount of money worth it to have that kind of pain? I guess so when you are trying to put yourself through college or needing to feed a family.

Back in the meat department and deli, it could get even more serious with the risks of meat slicers, hot ovens, and knives, etc. There have been mad dashes to the hospital for a finger that seemed to disappear. Can you believe that if a finger gets cut off and they can't sew it back on, you can receive a hefty settlement? What a terrible thought! Burns are common, usually on the arms. Third-degree burns can leave a nasty scar and mostly happen on the forearms and not on the face, thankfully.

Now the first aid kits at the market left a lot to be desired. They usually couldn't be found or if they were there wasn't anything in them. So, Cindy from the deli, decided to do something about it in an attempt to rack up some brownie points with the owner. She was getting way too many customer complaints these days and really wanted to do something for free on her own time. One day she asked the big boss, the head honcho, if she could go around and make sure all of the first aid kits were up to snuff. He said, sure, why not, but didn't sound too impressed. He figured the deli must be slow and she just needed some busy work.

She came in on a Tuesday on her day off and got all eight of the empty kits together and left the store. Six hours later, with her job complete, they were full of bandages, gauze pads, eye wash solution, burn cream, and aspirin. She even called the Red Cross to get a list of items to include. She put them in all of the areas of the store; the bakery, floral department, the deli, the front end where the check stands were, the back end where the dairy cases were, upstairs in the break room, and the office area.

One week later, the boss, the owner, the head honcho, came around the corner of the break room and smack-down hit his head on the corner of the table as he tripped and fell to the floor. A head injury bleeds a lot because there is no muscle, just skin and bone until you get into the brain part, so that little cut was amazing. Everyone was screaming and yelling and Cindy was called from the deli because deep down she always had a secret desire to be a doctor. She walked quickly upstairs into the horror of the sight of blood everywhere and everybody was trying to do something about it.

"Call 911!" She said. "Get back, all of you get back!! Give him some space!"

She laid him down on the break room couch, elevated his legs, grabbed the first aid kit which she knew was full, pulled out some gauze bandages and rubber gloves and proceeded to apply pressure with her gloved hand to the bosses' forehead. She looked like she was consoling "the thinker". She asked him if he had a headache. It all happened very fast and finally the bleeding stopped. A bandage was applied and when the paramedics arrived they took him in just to make sure he didn't have a concussion. Thankfully, he didn't. He was back to work the very next day with two stitches in his head.

He called Cindy into his office and said he'd really been impressed with her work at the store, including her performance under pressure the previous day.

"There had been a couple of customer complaints, but it's hard to please everybody. We can only do our best," he said. "I know you are trying to do your best...and about yesterday, when you asked if you could fill those first aid kits, I thought it was a good idea but we have all of those things on the shelves. All we have to do is run out there and get it. However, your proactive thinking of filling the first aid kits and having everything ready and accessible was spot on. I had no idea I would be the one using it first. Thank God, it was clear up here! And thank God, you took the initiative to do something that was not even asked of you!"

He looked her right in the eye and said those words that everybody longs to hear from their boss; those simple little words that make you fly like an eagle. Two words, "Good job!"

She stood up and smiled, thanked him, and felt 10-feet off the ground for the rest of her shift. It was simply amazing to realize the positive or negative impact we all have on each other. Let's face it, it feels great to be recognized for something positive.

Product Sampling

Mandy went to work every day with a smile on her face and lit up the world around her. Jason, in produce, flashed his amazing smile and everyone left that department with a beautiful basket of brightly colored fruits and vegetables and a whole lot of good vibes. Those were the people that brightened people's lives and it never hurt to tell them they're doing a good job. So, if you personally know someone who waits on you, yes it's their job, but if they do it well, please tell them. It doesn't cost you anything but is valuable to them.

The self-serve salad bar by the deli isn't free. You've seen those people over in the bulk foods section, you know the ones, the "grazers." They are just human chipmunks with their cheeks full of snacks picked out with greasy fingers from the bins. They are the penny pinchers who just take, take, and take. We've all seen them help themselves, it's basically stealing! Somehow they justify it in their heads because, well let's face it, everybody does it. If they didn't want people to do it, they wouldn't have it out there in the open. You often see people load up a pound of chocolate covered pretzels in a bag and then walk around the store, shopping and snacking as they go so that by the time they get to the checkout line they only have to pay for ½ pound instead of the original one pound.

It's disgusting. People literally help themselves to strawberries on the salad bar. They are easy to pick up and pop into your mouth. Cherry tomatoes, carrots, you name it. They should be ashamed, which brings up food demonstrations. The market had them every Friday and every department had something to demo; the bakery had cake, the deli demo consisted of dips and crackers, and the meat department had meatballs. You could literally eat breakfast, lunch and dinner there, in fact many people did!

Everyone kept track of their demos and it had to be deducted from inventory because obviously they didn't sell that product and gave it away. Very rarely did they sell more of the product than what they demonstrated so it was pretty much a wash. It's just another way to satisfy the customers.

Carrie had just put out a platter with about a hundred slices of marble fudge cake in little paper cups and she came back five minutes later to find that they were all gone. *That was quick! So, they liked it did they?* She thought to herself. She decided to put out a pumpkin pie that had burned around the edges, but they would never know because she'd cut that part off. She put them out and came back 10 minutes later to find them all still there except one or two. *Ok, they don't like pumpkin pie today.*

Barb was putting out samples of spinach dip. Nobody seemed to want anything to do with it. Maybe spinach sounded too healthy so she put out some homemade salsa and chips instead. Within ten minutes, it was gone! The salsa was dripping over the side of the glass bowl, down the side of the salad case, and onto the floor making a huge mess! Salsa drips easily and maybe not the best thing for a demo. Barb then chose some cheese from the cheese table. She cut it up into small cubes, put out some toothpicks, and in walked Daniel, a local musician/bum who was always in the store "grazing" in the bulk food section.

He smiled his sheepish little grin at Barb and asked, "Well, what do we have here?"

"Cheese. Pepper Jack." Barb answered curtly.

"Well, let's have a taste." Daniel said.

He reached in for a piece and apparently liked it enough to reach in for another one, and then another one. Barb thought to herself that this was pathetic. Imagine, a grown man living off the samples in the market. He thanked her for the snack and grabbed a napkin, and put three more pieces of cheese on it.

He said, "I'll be back to buy some of that cheese once I get paid next week."

Barb knew he wouldn't be back to buy anything except maybe a dozen eggs or a six pack of beer from time to time. He picked up his basket as if he was off to go shopping and sauntered over to the next sample station. He was there every sample Friday. He put a few things in his basket, hit all the sample stations, and then left his basket of items by the exit door as he left. Barb was glad she was not married to that, and at least he didn't "steal".

Then there was Mrs. Carmichael who came in on demo day, took little bites of everything, and helped herself to lots more. She left her wrappers and sample cups all over the floor and even in the aisles. One of the front parcel young men usually would follow her trail around the store, picking up her garbage. It didn't matter that each demo station had a garbage can positioned right there, few people actually used them. People most often would just get their toothpick and sample, or their little napkin and walk away. Then, since they walked away from the garbage can, they would just stick it on a random shelf or drop it nonchalantly on the floor. It was very annoying.

Joe, the janitor, really disliked demo day because it meant more scuff marks on the floor and more litter to pick up. It resulted in more work for everybody, but the owner of the store knew he made a lot of new friends and kept the old ones. "Make new friends, but keep the old, one is silver and the other gold," as the song goes.

So, once a month, on a Saturday, the market lived through demo day! Everyone who worked in the store on that day knew they'd be paying their dues for coming in late or calling in sick. The ones who did call in sick were usually the greenhorns who had seniority and had asked for it off long in advance. On one particular demo day, the owner was getting ready to take a trip to Greece. While he was away, the Assistant Manager, Frank, would make all the decisions and handle all of the problems that may arose from customers, employees, or whatever. He was not looking forward to it!

Peter's Revenge

An employee named Peter is worth mentioning. Peter used to work in the deli and a prior to that he was dating Cindy. She didn't even know that Peter had applied to work in the deli, but he did and the charmer and manipulator that he was, they hired him. When he was asked if he knew anyone in the deli, he lied and said no, but said that he'd frequented the deli many times over the years and thought it was the best deli in town. He added that he'd be honored to work there. Of course the deli department manager took this as a huge compliment to his ego and so it was done and Peter went to work in the deli.

Peter was kind of an odd looking duck, balding fast with a very large head! He walked pigeon-toed, just to try to look cute, and his best friend was his dog. Peter had been addicted to many things over the years. He learned fast in the deli and gave incredible customer service, but he was very slow when it came to production such as making dips, salads, cleaning, and cooking. He did it on his own time which sometimes, most of the time, just didn't work. However, he gave great customer service, especially to the women.

Peter was a total flirt! He had run his own gardening business in the past and he came to work at the deli to find all of those poor, or should we say, rich, elderly women who not only needed their yard mowed, but occasionally needed errands run or something heavy lifted, you get the picture. Peter was paid well, under the table, of course. Cash, up front. Even baked goods came his way for all of his good intentions.

Peter was driving Cindy crazy and she asked not to work with him. Her request was met with, "Cindy, I know you better than that. You can rise above whatever happened between you and Peter and just make this all about work. Remember, it's not good to bring your personal life to work so this will be a good test for you."

Yeah right, Cindy thought. *A real test to see how much I can put up with before I go crazy. I guess it doesn't matter that I've been here for years. I guess my requests don't mean anything.*

One day, Peter was bringing out a pan of chicken that took him 15 minutes to unload into the serving pan for the hot case. Cindy knew that the chicken temperature was falling dangerously low. Chicken has to stay warm and needs to cook to 165-170 degrees and then needs to stay at 145-150 to be served as "hot chicken". As usual, Peter was messing around and talking with one of the new hires back in the deli, a girl of course, and just did not care about the chicken temperature at all.

Cindy said, "The dinner rush is about to start and we better get that chicken into the case." Peter flipped out.

"Don't be telling me what to do! I know perfectly well what I'm doing and I want you off my back!" He called for the PIC and the plot began to get rid of Cindy from the store forever.

Weeks went by without incident and a vacancy for a checker position opened up at the front of the store. Peter wanted it. It paid more than the deli and he wouldn't have to clean up, cook chicken, and do "women's work." The department you worked in had to make a recommendation in order to move from one department to another and even though the deli department manager was not that impressed with Peter's speed, he knew that he did give great customer service so he said yes. He recommended Peter for the position and added that he would be a great person to have up front, knowing full well that it might help to relieve a lot of tension back in the deli.

Peter had been working up front for about six months when Cindy took a leave of absence to have an operation. While she was recovering,

Peter's conscious got the best of him. He loved it when a woman was weak and vulnerable so he showed up with flowers at Cindy's house and wanted to know how she was feeling. Then, he dropped the bomb! He told Cindy, in confidence, that he had been stealing money from the cash register. Cindy, in the midst of trying to heal and drowsy from medication, took it all in. Since she was not currently working at the store, she decided to try not to get involved with that big can of worms!

Cindy told Peter he needed to stop stealing before he got caught and that nothing good could come of it.

"Why did you even tell me?" Cindy yelled. "I wish you had never told me. Thank you for the flowers, but I'm tired now. You need to leave."

Cindy closed the door behind Peter and had to sit down. Her head was spinning from hearing this information. She didn't see Peter for another three weeks after his surprise visit.

When she did finally go back to work, it was unbearable. Every time Cindy had to walk by the front of the store and see Peter standing there in the checkout counter, she wondered every day, if he was still taking money from the register. She then made a big mistake by asking a coworker what to do if she had information about someone stealing from the store. She didn't know whether or not to tell her boss, so she asked her coworker, thinking it was only between the two of them. The coworker agreed that it was a bad position to be in and then headed to the break room. There were three people already sitting there, eating their snacks.

The coworker turned to them and said,"Hey, Cindy just asked me the strangest question. She wondered what I would do if someone came to me personally and admitted that they were stealing from the store."

Peter was one of the three people in the break room. He couldn't believe his ears! It sounded to him like Cindy was considering turning him in. Maybe she wouldn't do that, but he was going to find out!

Peter showed up at Cindy's house that night and threatened her.

"You keep your big mouth shut or you'll regret it!" He shouted. She couldn't believe it! Not only did her co-worker betray her trust and blab her big mouth, but Peter would never trust her again. He was the one stealing and yet he was threatening her.

The next morning she went to her deli manager and said, "I need to talk to you and Frank." Frank was the assistant manager. By then it was too late. Apparently Peter had been up all night plotting Cindy's fate. He had gotten other deli workers, who didn't like Cindy, to put in writing that she had harassed them at work and made it uncomfortable for them to be there. They accused her of creating a 'hostile work environment'.

Cindy was called into the office. She thought it was going to be a conversation with her manager and the assistant store manager. She thought this would be the moment of truth. She wanted to let them know that she didn't want any part of Peter's conscience on her shoulders but what she was met with were three words. Peter had done his homework and called the union to make sure these three words would do exactly what they did; get Cindy fired!

She sat there in total disbelief knowing that Peter had said to keep her mouth shut, or else. Well, the "or else" came sooner that she thought it would! She slowly stood up knowing that she would wait until the store owner came back from his trip and then she'd let him know what happened. She also knew that with all of the customer complaints and how she was now feeling about the store, she didn't want to work there anymore anyway.

Cindy had two teenage boys to feed and a mortgage, but enough was enough. That was the last straw. If her co-workers could be so easily persuaded to attack her, then she was done! She went on unemployment, stated exactly what had happened, told everything she knew about Peter on her report and waited for the owner to come back to town. They had always had a working relationship of mutual respect. When they finally met, he listened to her entire story and together, they decided it was best if she found employment elsewhere, which she did.

Six months later, Peter had a nervous breakdown in the check stand and had to go on extended leave. He did not get to collect unemployment so what goes around, comes around. Karma. That's how the story goes. Ah yes, life at the market! All of the incredible people, the team work, the bonding, the laughs, the customers, the incredible food, the beautiful flowers, and the work, work, work!

It takes a certain breed to choose that life. Some people have a college degree, others don't. Some are happy working at the market for 30 plus years, others aren't. Every town has one, or many, and the competition is fierce in the larger towns and cities where there may be a market every six to eight blocks. However, it's a necessity. They provide communities with consumables we all need to survive and they provide jobs to support families. You just don't realize the drama behind the scenes!

Chicken Soup for the Heart & Soul

How do people choose which market to go to? Many think it's the store's prices, other people shop by location and the one that is closest to their home. In the wake of rising gas prices, it certainly does play into it. Others believe it's all about the customer service and the cleanliness of the store. It could be a combination of all of the above. Certainly, the days of getting the newspaper and looking through the sales are over. You remember, or maybe you don't, getting all those newspaper ads in the Sunday paper and seeing who had bananas on sale or the cheapest eggs. You went there to buy those things and then headed over to another store across town for toilet paper that was twenty cents cheaper.

Supposedly, the third best place to meet a mate is while shopping. With everyone on their cell phones these days, walking around with lists of what they need to buy, who has time to look up, or stop and talk long enough to actually meet a perspective companion. Actually, it does happen and Ruth and John were living proof.

Ruth was in the soup aisle looking for a can of mushroom soup for her "world famous" scalloped potato recipe. John was in the same aisle looking pretty dazed and confused. Ruth bent over to pick up the can, of course it was on the bottom shelf, and when she stood back up, John was reaching for a can of chicken noodle soup three shelves above her. He never meant to hurt Ruth, not in a thousand years, but the hand with the soup can in it came right down on top of her head as she stood upright! He clunked her head pretty good and for a moment she saw stars and then realized she was ok as her eyes fought to re-focus.

John profusely apologized for his negligence and Ruth was looking into the eyes of a man she realized had been in her dreams for the last two years. Both John and Ruth were in their early 40's, had both been married, each had a grown child and were as lonely as Hell! Ruth told John she was ok, no worries, but she could see by his red nose and eyes that he was suffering from a bad cold.

Ruth cooked a lot and knew the value of garlic. She told John it would be a good idea for him to go over to the produce and get some garlic to add to his soup. Ruth made everything from scratch and she found herself asking the man, she didn't know his name yet, if he lived in this part of town. She was very bold because she didn't see a wedding ring, and she was lonely.

He replied that yes, he did, he had just moved to town. Ruth's heart was pounding, her head didn't hurt at all anymore, and in fact she couldn't feel any part of her body. She found herself asking him for his address because she wanted to make him some of her homemade chicken soup. He couldn't believe his ears! First, he knocked this beautiful woman over the head with a can of soup and now, by the grace of God, she was offering him homemade soup! Who was she, he wondered? He loved her! It was love at first sight. He was in love with her Spirit!

John pulled out a business card and was a little bit excited because he hadn't been on a date in almost two years and he was a little rusty. He reminded himself not to look too desperate. He asked if she had a pen so he could write his home phone number on the back of the business card. She flipped it over and saw that he was a home improvement carpenter. She smiled back and said she was really busy but in the next couple of days she would be showing up with the soup. She knew he wouldn't be getting that much better from the canned chicken soup anytime soon. They said goodbye and both left the soup aisle humming the same song, "I've been waiting so long." by Journey.

Ruth showed up at John's house exactly two days later. She called before she went just to make sure he was there. His home was beautiful with lots of hardwoods, stained glass, and everything she loved. Ruth was an interior designer and she thought to herself as she told John what she did for a living how this union could be exactly what the doctor ordered. Well, cut to three years later, after John and Ruth dated for a year, then he sold his home and together they built the most incredible "nest."

Some people do shop at markets and wind up leaving with more than just their groceries. There isn't a day that goes by that John doesn't give thanks to the market and being at the right place at the right time. The market catered the wedding and took care of everything from the flowers, to the food, to the cake, and every anniversary after that.

Each year, Ruth made John a big pot of homemade chicken noodle soup (with garlic) and they sat and laughed, and laughed, and laughed as all couples in love should do. All of those happy encounters, all of those not-so-happy encounters, every day was a new day at the market and, like most days, no one really knew what it would bring. It could be happiness, joy, excitement, terror, it could never be predicted. In the back of the bakery, on the employee bulletin board, there was a sign that read, "When things get rough, tie a knot and HOLD ON!"

The Salmonella Scare

The BIG S.S.!

Jason, in produce, had taken a trip to Mexico and while he was there he had a great time drinking margaritas, going parasailing and taking in the many restaurants. He had a blast, but what he didn't know was that while he was there, he had picked up salmonella. Salmonella, as you probably know, is a bacterial disease and very contagious.

Not knowing he had salmonella, he returned home and went back to work at the market. The second week he was home, he got very sick. Jason never traveled and even though he had a great time, and never got sick there like many people do, he was definitely sick then. He went to the doctor and they ran many tests and finally found out the cause of his illness. The major problem was that he had gone back to work and handled a lot of produce, which could have spread to any of the shoppers, customers, and employees in those first two weeks that he'd been back.

What was the market to do? The owner was advised by the Health Department that they would have to run an ad in the local paper stating the dates that Jason was working and that anybody who bought food there may have been exposed and should see their doctor or go to the Health Department to be tested for salmonella right away. They had to nip this in the butt before the whole town got infected. What a mess!

The store was definitely losing business over it even though Jason was home on sick leave. The cat had to be let out of the bag. There just wasn't any other way around it. By law, if you worked with the public, you had to notify the public of any health risk. Jason felt terrible for many reasons. Not only was he very sick for about 15 days, but what the market had to go through was incredible. About 400 people ran, not walked, to their healthcare providers, but not one case appeared. However, it had to be done. That year was very rough on the market. The doors almost closed for good due to the cost of having to cover all the tests and health exams.

Jason felt so guilty for bringing this on at his place of work, that he vowed never to go to Mexico again, and he never had a margarita since! He didn't, to this day, know where he got the salmonella from and he probably never would.

Some customers will look for years for someone to sue so that they can live their life in the lap of luxury! It was quite a day at the market. It was raining softly and an unusually busy day. There were no holidays at the time and the departments were all running smoothly. Life was good at the market on that day until…Nancy Smith ran out of milk while she was making tapioca pudding.

Nancy pulled up and parked in the parking lot. She got out of her car and made a run for the door. The rain had gotten a little steadier and she had just gotten her hair done. She didn't really want to get wet, so she was moving pretty fast. The automatic door opened for her and she hustled inside the market. The carpet that was placed by the doors helped to keep the floor a little cleaner and Joe the Janitor really thought it was a good idea. People could wipe their feet off, just like being at home. *Better yet*, Joe thought, *why didn't they just leave their shoes outside?* No, that would have been too much to ask.

Nancy ran in to grab a basket and caught the edge of her shoe on the corner of the carpet and down she went right onto her right knee and hand. At that moment, Cathy from the bakery was walking by and saw her fall. She ran to her side and could tell she was in definite pain. Cathy called for help but Nancy did not want to go to the hospital because she had no health insurance and no idea what it would all cost. She had no idea that her decision would have very dire consequences.

Nancy was lying on the floor clutching her knee and it felt to her like her knee cap had fallen off. She just held onto it and wouldn't let anyone look at it. When the paramedics finally arrived, she eased her hand away reluctantly. What they found was that her knee was still intact, but badly bruised. There was, however, a small hole. A rock, dragged inside the store by the bottom of someone's shoe, had lodged inside her knee. The paramedics wanted to take her in for an x-ray, but she refused. They insisted that it needed to be done just to be sure everything was ok. So she finally agreed to get the x-ray and $500 later, she was sent home. The store paid for half because they did feel it was somewhat their responsibility, although she was running in bad weather conditions.

For about a week, Nancy couldn't bend her knee. She got so frustrated; she called her doctor who said she needed to come back in so he could check for infection. The doctor drained the fluid out of her knee which eased the swelling and discomfort. Feeling better, she went on a trip to California for a week where the weather was warmer. Low and behold, she contracted a rare soft tissue disease that re-infected her leg and again, it become very inflamed and painful.

Nancy went to an emergency room in California and they administered a shot directly into her knee to treat the infection. The tragic thing was that she had an allergic reaction to the shot and died. Things like this you can never predict. You can try using a Ouija board, or go to a palm reader, but life takes us all up and down and all around. Where is stops, nobody ever knows.

Nancy didn't have any children or any living family but her funeral service was full of many people she had touched over the years, including about half of the employees from the market who felt very badly about what had happened. Lesson learned, live each day as if it were your last. Tell the people in your life that you love them a lot so that when it's time to go you are clear to fly.

The American Way

Life goes on and at the market this was no exception. Deliveries were still made every day except for Sundays, people would come and go, but one thing is for sure, every town across the United States, and in most parts of the world have a market. It's part of life and survival when we need food, unless you grow your own. We need laundry detergent, unless you make your own. We need everything that is in the market.

Strolling down the aisles, you'd see people with their carts loaded to the brim for a family of three or four. You'd walk the aisles looking for excitement and intrigue; anything that jumped out at you sometimes you just had to have it! It's the American way. Those new cookies you saw an ad for on T.V. the other night; the new air fresheners with all the great scents from cookie dough to cedar trees. How can anyone resist them, especially those easy-to-grab items that line the check stands with magazines and candy and gum?

If you've ever witnessed a new mother who is standing in line with their four year old sitting in the cart at just the right level ransacking the boxes of rot-your-teeth candy because he's bored waiting, you know he wants every single colorful package he can get his little hands on! He picks them up, throws them into the cart, or into his pockets, or worse; opens them up and puts them straight into his mouth while mommy isn't paying attention! No matter what, Mom has to pay for them.

Why stores don't put books or toothbrushes or other healthier options in those check-out stands is a mystery. It's the ultimate tease! When did our instinctual needs become so much more? When did the food groups get replaced with egocentric, emotional items and create an allover sense of confusion? If we look back through the history of stores, we will see that as communities popped up all over, people needed and wanted a place to go and trade what they had for what they needed. Today, we kill ourselves to go purchase those "needed" items. Gone are the days where people shop from need lists to want lists. We make purchases out of an emotional void. We still get what we need but so much more creating a very wasteful and hoard-prone society. We work hard and then we reward ourselves by spending money, which brings us to the story of Ben and Reneé Glover.

Ben and Reneé

Ben worked at one of the local refineries and Reneé was an administrative assistant. They had no children and one dog, Benjamin. Ben and Reneé pretty much lived separate lives when they were unable to have children. Reneé desperately wanted kids so Ben went out a bought her a puppy. That puppy became a full grown dog and had every dog product on the market; chew toys, doggy treats, fifteen to twenty collars and ate only the best dog food. They spent $50.00 for an 11 lb. bag of dog food every week!

When Ben went shopping at the market, he always went straight to the pet aisle to see if there was something new that Benjamin needed to have. Inevitably he would come home with something new and before long, the second bedroom of their two-bedroom home was filled with every dog product imaginable. Benjamin fulfilled Ben's desires for a child, but it wasn't quite the same for Reneé. She collected salt-and-pepper shakers! She was up to about 457 pairs.

Most couples will call each other up around 4:00 pm and talk about what they'd like to have for dinner, or just ask how things were going in general. However neither Ben nor Reneé cooked, so the big question was always if they were eating in or out. Most of the time they'd agree to eat out and then it was a question of where. If they decided to eat in, then it was a question of ordering in or picking something out of the freezer.

They had two freezers; one filled with every frozen food available from the market; macaroni and cheese, pot stickers, pot pies, frozen pizza, frozen TV dinners, frozen cakes, fish sticks, French fries, frozen lasagna, you name it. They had enough frozen food to survive for at least six months. When they shopped at the market they'd go right to the pet aisle, the frozen food aisle, and the paper product/cleaning supply aisle, and that's about it. The other freezer, believe it or not, was mostly empty in case the full freezer went on the blink. They also had a back-up generator in case the power went out for more than 24 hours. They didn't want to lose all of their food, plus they could plug the microwave into the generator power, cook their frozen food, and never have to worry about powering up the stove!

Whenever Ben and Reneé would come by the coffee shop, Mandy would tell them about the frozen foods on sale that week. They always appreciated that but sometimes it would back-fire since they never shopped together. There was the time Ben bought ten bags of frozen strawberries and then two hours later, Renee did too and they had to break down and use the second freezer to fit them all in.

You can tell a lot about an individual by what they eat. The checkers at the market got pretty amused with the different combinations of items. Greg, who works at the store, the beer guy, wished he knew more about cooking and diet and never hesitated when he saw fresh fish and maybe some fettuccine, and broccoli going through the register to ask the customer what they might be doing with the ingredients. He'd gotten a lot of recipe ideas over the years but he still stuck to his usual meat and potatoes.

The head coach of the local university football team was in the market at least three times a week ordering up those big rib eye steaks from Matt, just the way he liked them. He went home and burned the hell out of them on his BBQ. The market was seeing more and more weight conscious customers cutting back on the sugar and fatty foods as folks were trying to eat more sensibly by adding vegetables and more whole grains to their diets. This prompted the store owner to add an organic section to the store which in turn had once again brought in some new shoppers to the market.

Those folks used to be called "hippies" or "granola heads" and would usually smell of lavender oil, sandalwood, or patchouli. They were typically very happy people, high on life, but most likely high on something else. Then there were the folks who were on the opposite end of the spectrum and were extremely athletic and super health conscious. They worked out three times, or more per week, counted calories, and lived mainly on fruits and vegetables often made into smoothies with some protein powder mixed in.

Organic food is not cheap. Foods grown and raised with all the additive sprays, insecticides, colorings, etc. cost less because they can be mass-produced on huge farms with a lot of machinery and chemicals. Organic food is grown without all of that so-called technology, and most of it is grown locally by small farmers on their privately owned land. They have to obtain special certification, which is very costly, and there are inspections to pass which also have a fee associated with them. The food is filled with a lot more vitamins and minerals to help us all stay healthy, but you tend to have to pay a little extra for it.

The organic food was labeled as such, and unfortunately customers had been known to take labels off the regular, non-organic items, and put them onto the organic items in order to pay less. For example, regular bananas are $0.79 per pound while organic bananas are $1.79 per pound. If they could get away with it, they would take off the tape that says "organic" to save an extra dollar. Anyone who is in the habit of not paying full price for organic food should really think twice as they are only screwing over the organic farmers and taking away from the local economy, not to mention they are also ripping off the market and biting the hand that feeds them.

Raven

Raven entered the market. She was twenty-two years old with long, dark, matted hair and many piercings. She was wearing a long, flowing skirt with every color of the rainbow woven into the pattern. She walked up to the front check stand to ask where the organic section was. One of the front courtesy clerks asked her what she was looking for and explained that the organic products were in one section of the store but the organic produce was over by the regular produce.

She looked a little confused by the information she received but figured she'd still go and explore anyway. Her mind was somewhat fuzzy from the chocolate mushroom treats she had taken the night before and she wondered if eating organically might do her some good while she spent much of her time polluting her mind with her experimental drugs, just to "enlighten" herself.

She headed over to aisle four where she started looking for organic black beans, rice milk, and generally anything that said "organic" on it. She happened to run into her old friend Jeremy who she used to see a lot on the music festival circuit.

Jeremy asked, "Have you heard about the party tonight over at Tim's?

"No, I haven't. I just got back from Mexico and have been kind of out of the loop." Raven answered.

"Well, there's going to be a D.J. and five dancers, belly dancers! It's going to be a blast! You should go!" Jeremy said.

"Thanks for the info. I might but right now I'm hungry and can't really think about much else." Raven put two cans of organic canned corn into her basket along with the organic black beans.

Jeremy gave her a hug and continued on his merry way. Raven thought to herself that life has all these clubs and social groups; same ol' same ol'. Her life included all sorts of clubs and groups; the religious fanatics, the health nuts, the blue collar workers, white collar workers, artists, musicians, etc. Everybody thinks they are druggies and alcoholics and part of the in-crowd. It just depends what you're into. Some people cross over into more than one group but in general, where their interests are is where they 'hang'.

Raven was trying to remember what else she was looking for at the store. Even when you're young, the more drugs you do, the less you can remember things. She hated this feeling of not being able to remember even the simplest of things like what to buy at the store. She decided right there and then, on aisle four, that at the ripe old age of 22 she had had enough. No more drugs for her. Except now she would have to find a new club! It would be hard leaving her "drug club" where she made so many great friends, but she knew she'd be ok. She made friends easily.

Speaking of making new friends easily, at that moment, walking down the organic food aisle was a nice looking young man looking very clean, sharp, and down to Earth. Raven wondered for a second if she should say hello since he probably wouldn't even respond to her wearing a rainbow skirt and her hair that she would soon be cutting off. However, she mustered up the courage and very casually said, "hey, how are you?"

On this particular day, the young man was taken aback that anyone would be asking him how he's doing but he answered back, "I'm good, how are you?"

Raven said, "Really good, I just decided to change my life today." She smiled.

The young man said, "Great! That's always a good thing." He smiled back at her.

Paul was 24 and attending school to work with troubled teenagers. He didn't do drugs and he played outside a lot; tennis, kayaking, attending music festivals, stuff like that. Everything he got involved in, he did with a clear head, clean, and straight. Raven believed that meeting Paul, in that moment, in the organic food aisle, was cosmic. It was divine intervention. It was destiny. On the very day, at the very moment she made the decision to change her life around, Paul walked into it.

Paul asked Raven if she was interested in going to grab a cup of coffee or tea, or perhaps a smoothie across the street at the café.

"That would be incredibly great!" She answered back with a smile. Her heart was beaming. They put down their shopping baskets and walked out of the market, neither one of them wanted to wait to purchase anything. They seized the moment and the momentum. Raven did not want to risk losing the chance to get to know this angel who would help her get her life back together in the healthiest way.

The Good, the Bad, and the Ugly!

Some days start out so terribly wrong! Take, for example, one Sunday being the largest day of the week for newspaper circulation, when Greg came in to open the store at 6:00 a.m., there was not a single paper by the front door. Knowing there would be hundreds of people coming through who would want one, he got on the phone within two minutes of walking in the door to find out that the papers had been delivered at 3:00 a.m. and if they weren't there, well, somebody must have stolen them!

Greg was panicking as he dashed back out the front door and looked up and down the street to see that the bundle of papers had come open somehow and about three hundred newspapers were flying around and strewed all over the street and parking lot! How had he missed that when he was walking in the first time?

Just great! Greg thought, as he wondered whether or not to call someone in early to start picking up this mess. The wind was blowing and the papers were scattering off into neighbor's yards, up into trees and bushes, and finding their way onto parked cars on the street. Then, the worst happened. It started to rain! Things went from good, to bad, to ugly pretty darn quick!

The rain was making the papers stick to things and they were falling apart. He wasn't sure what to do. He called the newspaper dispatch to ask if they could deliver more papers right away and he explained the bale had become unsecured and he wasn't sure how this happened. The litter was extensive, he further explained, and he'd be at the store for another half hour, alone, before anyone else would come on shift.

The newspaper dispatch said they would send out another bale of papers as soon as they could and if he could get someone out there to help with the clean-up then they would too. Greg hung up the phone and tried to think of who he could call but no one came to mind. *Think, think, think…*

Suddenly, he had an idea. He hated to do it, but he thought of Joe. Joe was retired but Greg knew how much he absolutely hated litter and dirt. He dialed Joe's number.

"Hi, this is Greg at the market. Sorry for waking you up so early but I've got a real problem down here. We've got a wild bale of newspapers that are blowing up and down the block. The newspaper company is sending someone down to help clean it up but I need to get someone in here too to help. I thought of you. Can you come in as soon as possible?"

Greg wasn't getting anywhere with Joe when Cindy walked in to open up the deli. Greg covered up the phone and said to Cindy, "Joe is on the line and I need him to come in and help clean up these wild newspapers blowing all over the place." Cindy motioned to hand her the phone.

"Joe, this is Cindy. Hi! Can you believe this guy calling you early on a Sunday morning to come and help clean up the street?" Cindy smirked.

"No, I sure as hell can't, Cindy!" Joe said.

"Well, it's unbelievable, but if you come in he says he'll give you $50 for one hour of work and some of our chicken from the deli for free. You just tell us how much you want," said Cindy.

Joe started to weaken. "Ok," he said. "I'll be right there."

He was at the market in fifteen minutes with one of those poles with a nail on it and within one hour the whole, hot mess was cleaned up! Joe went home $50.00 richer and with a 24-piece bucket of free chicken that he was really not supposed to eat since he just had open heart surgery.

Valentine's Day

There are always two sides to every story. Virginia had been working at the market for almost thirty years. She loved her job, like Mandy in the coffee hutch. Virginia knew everyone and counseled everyone too. Once again, if you were in a hurry, it was not a good idea to get in her line! Repeat; do not get in her line! She talked more that anyone or everybody in the whole store combined.

Most people loved Virginia, but some people hated or disliked her with a passion. It was best to take her with a grain of salt, as my grandfather would always say. If you needed advice, go through her line and she would tell you what you should be eating, who you should be romantically involved with, how many vitamins you should be taking, and what car you should be driving. In short, she was going to tell you exactly what you should be doing with your life, for free!

One amazing fact about Virginia was that she knew everybody's first name. For the customer lacking in attention, they would go through Virginia's line, have a good chat, and walk away wondering if you should listen to the dear old gal, or just forget everything she just told them. Most people did a little of both because it would be completely unwise to not listen to the wise woman, at least with a grain of salt.

Virginia had been married three times, had four children, and worked since she was twelve years old. At age 62, perhaps she felt qualified, with all of her life experience, to give unsolicited advice to strangers, or anyone who would listen. Like Mandy, she spent an untold amount of time listening to customers. For example, there was Martha, who was 21 years old and had never been on a date or kissed by a member of the opposite sex.

Martha had found her way into Virginia's line as a meek brunette with glasses and a very unattractive, baggy fashion sense. On Valentine's Day, Virginia could sense by the look on the poor, pathetic girl's face that she was not in the happiest of moods. She was buying sanitary pads and a pack of chewing gum and was completely embarrassed by her purchase. It was written all over her face. There was a man in front of her in line, and one behind her, but she chose Virginia's line because she was the only female checker on shift and she couldn't bear to go through a male-checker's line that day. Especially on Valentine's Day of all days!

Virginia could sense her restlessness and knew she wanted to hurry up and get out of there. Earlier in the day, someone had given her a big Hershey's kiss to thank her for the many years of friendship and great advice, but not everyone felt that way about Virginia. When it was finally Martha's turn to pay for her items, Virginia quietly asked how she was doing.

Martha replied, "Ok."

"Any Valentine's Day plans for tonight? Virginia winked and smiled.

At that moment, all of the anxiety, hormones, and self-consciousness caught up with her and she exploded with, "No! I don't have a boyfriend, ok?" She was really just hoping Virginia would quickly put her things into a bag and let her leave, but no, in her usual nosey way, she continued. Tears started to form in the corners of her eyes and she could feel her face getting hot and red. She looked like a wounded bird trying to get away from the cat that was tormenting it.

With that, Virginia went into action.

"Well, you know you have very beautiful eyes and you should get some contact lenses and I don't believe in women looking like strippers but

I bet if you wore something a little more fitted…" Virginia looked her up and down from across the check stand, "…you look like you're in great shape! If you've got it, why not flaunt it? I don't know why you don't have a boyfriend. You look healthier and more attractive than a lot of young girls I see with their noses all pierced up and tattoos all over their body, and the crazy outfits they wear!" As she rambled on, Martha was averting her eyes, growing more embarrassed by the minute.

Virginia slipped the big Hershey's kiss into Martha's grocery bag without her noticing. She finished her transaction, thanked Virginia, and hurried out of the store, bumping into an elderly man on her way. She swore to herself that she would never, ever, step foot in that market again. Well, February 14th rolled around the following year and Virginia was still working her regular 8:00 a.m. to 5:00 p.m. shift at the checkout stand and lo-and-behold, Martha found herself back in her line. Except, this time she was wearing contact lenses, had on a very beautiful red sweater which fit her curves nicely, and her hair was longer and very femininely tapered around her face. She was sporting an engagement ring!

She had two chocolate hearts from the bakery and a container of strawberries, some very expensive champagne and some bubble bath. Virginia looked up and said, "Somebody's going to have a good night! You lucky girl, or should I say lucky guy?"

Martha looked at Virginia with her beautiful eyes and said, "You don't remember me, do you?"

Virginia paused a moment, because she never forgot a face, then said, "I think I do remember you, sweetheart! But, refresh my memory."

Martha reminded her about the incident that had occurred exactly one year ago; about how she commented on her glasses, her clothes, her figure, and most importantly how she slipped the chocolate kiss inside her grocery bag. She explained how she ran home and sobbed all night. She ate the entire Hershey's kiss in one sitting and the next day she made an appointment at the hair salon and to get fitted for contact lenses. She went through her entire wardrobe, threw out half of it, and spent $500 dollars on new clothes, which was a lot for her to spend on herself, or anything really.

"Three weeks later, at the bank where I work, my boss asked me out!" Martha exclaimed. He was a young, responsible, healthy, loving, and giving man and they started dating. Martha shoved her left hand out in Virginia's face to show off her diamond engagement ring.

"We're getting married on July 20th, on his birthday, because he wanted to get married on the anniversary of the day we met because when he met me it was like he was born all over again! So, we are celebrating his birthday by getting married!"

Virginia was stunned. She stopped everything she was going, did the unthinkable and came out from behind the check stand to give Martha a great big hug. Martha took Virginia's hand and placed a Hershey's kiss in it.

"Thank you so much for telling me the truth that day, even though I was horrified at the time, but it truly did change my life. I would be honored if you would come to our wedding." Martha said with a big smile on her face.

"Of course I will come!" Virginia had tears in her eyes. "Thank you for making my Valentine's Day special this year!"

Not everyone has the nerve to say what they feel or what is in their heart. It's a risk because even with the best of intentions, we don't want to offend anyone. We don't mean to be hurtful, but sometimes a little push in the right direction and a little encouragement is all a person needs to help them change their lives forever. Thank God for people like Virginia.

Misunderstandings

Sometimes, saying the wrong thing at the wrong time causes a snowball effect. It can be disastrous! Virginia was working her usual shift, in her usual talkative way, when a woman came through her line to purchase cottage cheese, a pineapple, some bananas, coffee, and a quart of ice cream. Virginia, in her usual mode of incessant talking, giving out advice, and moving to the next customer, looked at the items on the conveyor belt and asked the very large woman before her when her baby was due.

Well, this was not the time or the place to say that because the woman was not pregnant. In fact, she had battled with her weight all her life and was, once again, on a diet. She was already feeling guilty about buying ice cream so when Virginia asked her when her baby was due, she lost it.

"I am here to purchase my items, which pays your salary, and I don't need your questions, your remarks, or your judgement. It's none of your business! By the way, I am NOT pregnant!" The woman stormed out of the store. The air was thick with her anger. It was as if a dark cloud rolled over check stand three.

The woman wrote a letter to the owner of the market complaining about the way she was treated by Virginia, saying that as long as she worked there she would never step foot in the store again. She went on to say she had told all her friends about what happened and they would also boycott the market. It was a very unfortunate situation and one Virginia had not meant any harm in. She honestly had good intentions, but it backfired severely and was one of those times when she crossed the line.

Everybody has their off days. Even the most emotionally intelligent person cannot be 100% right 100% of the time. Virginia wrote the woman an apology letter, but it didn't do any good. She received a note back from the woman telling Virginia to drop dead. Virginia had to chalk it up to a huge misunderstanding for which she felt very regretful. She really just wanted to forget it ever happened, like your 50th birthday or the day you run out of gas on the freeway in the middle of a huge downpour; raining so hard that nobody can even see you sitting there on the side of the road, waiting.

Have you ever noticed the music that is played in your local market? Well, how can you escape it? It's important to have good music to shop to. It only stands to reason that if the music is good, up-beat, happy, etc. you may keep your customers shopping and in your store longer. A smart store owner will pay his or her fees to the proper music distributors so they can actually play the original artist's music so that when you are listening, you are actually hearing the Beatles and not a bad re-make. Well, at this market, the owner was really behind the times. No offense, but Barry Manalo was not really popular anymore and the employees were about to go crazy forced to listen to it all day long; the same tracks over and over and over again.

They heard it in their sleep, they hummed "I sing the songs that make the whole world sing..." in their cars on their way home. It was getting to the point people were complaining about it a lot. Even customers were filing complaints about the music. At the monthly meeting, when the department heads were there, employees brought up the issue and asked if they would please consider playing different, more up to date, music in the store.

This was happening during the time the owner was on vacation for two weeks in Greece. He left specific instructions for the other managers, including what music to play. Apparently, his hand writing wasn't clear, or there was a miscommunication because the same tape was just put on repeat and never changed. For a full two weeks, the same tracks were played, over and over. Employees in the deli noticed a drop in business. They spent a lot of time there making salads, sandwiches, dips, and the like and needless to say, sales were down during those two weeks the owner was gone.

Many of the frequent shoppers had stopped coming regularly and couldn't be encouraged to stick around to have to hear continuous Trumpet music by Herb Alpert from the 60's. They tried to change the tracks manually on the sound system, but couldn't do it. They finally just turned it off for a couple of days, but that wasn't good either. Herb Alpert was better than silence. Finally, the owner called and was asked how to change the music. He said there was a code you had to input into the sound system before you could change the tracks. No wonder nobody could figure it out! Who would have thought there was a secret code? He was really touchy about the music, so no wonder he neglected to write it down, or tell anyone what the code was before he left.

Holiday Season at the Market

The holiday season starts long before Thanksgiving hits and one can find the red and white poinsettias lining the aisles, candy canes of all colors and flavors, window decals of snowflakes, snowmen, and Christmas trees started to appear quite early. The closer it got to Christmas, the more scenes that went up in the windows and displays; Santa with his reindeer, Frosty with his black hat and broomstick, and of course, more poinsettias.

Then there were the bell ringers. Ah the bell ringers! Before you even got inside the store, those people collecting money for the Salvation Army incessantly rang their bells standing right there as you were about to walk in, jumping up and down from the cold trying to stay warm. How could anyone walk past without putting in a few quarters, but many did. They just passed right by. Some really good bell-ringers had been known to raise up to $500 in a single day!

The checkers, however, could not wait for the holiday season to be over when they didn't have to listen to the constant bells ringing all of the time. Some had complained that they heard bells in their sleep for days after they have stopped, but it's a noble action standing there none the less. Sometimes they stood there for four to six hour shifts at a time, smiling, wishing everyone a Merry Christmas and trying their best not to seem to harassing by ringing that bell, over and over. Did they even feel their hands and feet after just a few hours? Did they have to go through some kind of training before getting that job?

The market also had a woman come and play her keyboard and sing Christmas carols every year. For seventeen years, that was one of her December gigs. She was 69 years old, very petite and she always wore a stocking hat that said Merry Christmas on it, red pants, a white down parka, and a big smile. She wore the exact same outfit every single year.

Mandy, from the deli, always saw to it that she got a cup of cocoa every two or three hours. She played inside the market just inside the doors between the shopping carts and the produce department. Virginia always felt sorry for her every time the doors opened and a big, cold draft would come sweeping through the front of the store, but the woman never complained.   When the market was sold and got new owners, she was asked to play outside. She didn't get paid. She did it because she enjoyed it, not for the money. Playing outside proved more challenging though. Not only because she was out in the cold, but because she had to compete with the constant bell ringing! However, she came to play out of the goodness of her heart. People tried to give her money, but she just pointed to the bell ringers and told them to put it in the bucket.

She smiled her million dollar smile and it lit up the whole world and everyone in it. She had a little white dog that faithfully sat by her side while she played. It was one of those Pekinese fluffy-looking, cute pups that just yaps and barks when you went to pet her. It would have been more fitting to have a friendlier dog there for her performance. She would play requests but didn't normally get to finish them because with all the coffee, tea, or cocoa Mandy was bringing her she made many breaks to the bathroom and the heated store, just because she needed to get out of the 40 degree weather.

Inside the market, all of the checkers wore Santa hats, flashing lights were on every check stand, cheery music played over the sound system, and it just felt like Christmas. It was a time of good cheer and amazement through a child's eyes or it could be a very sad time of year for those that had lost a loved one or for someone who was ill. The market owner did the best he could to keep a positive, festive atmosphere without overdoing it. The floral department had a lot of festive swags and wreathes decorated with every color bow imaginable to fit any décor. There was traditional holly, red bows, pine cones, and other not so traditional decorations too. There was white lace, baby's breath, and silver musical instruments. Don't forget the plaid ribbon, little bears with cute outfits on, something for everyone.

The market also brought in a lot of specialty wines, desserts, chocolates, anything and everything one's heart could desire during the holidays. One never knew if suddenly, when picking up the egg nog on the way to the family holiday party, you suddenly remembered that you forgot to get Aunt Ruth something so you go to the specialty gift aisle and pick up a nice box of uniquely wrapped Christmas candy so you don't have to run all the way back out to the mall. Or, maybe a set of new, tapered red candles, or some bath salts since she enjoyed baths so much.

Over in the bakery, where German Christmas Stolen was being prepared, there were fresh ginger bread house kits on display. One of the community's favorite holiday events was the night when families could come, buy a kit, and decorate a ginger bread house with gum drops, crushed Oreo cookies, marshmallows, candy canes, little pretzels, M&M's, cinnamon drops, and other little candies and sprinkles. The bakery employees loved it too because the children and parents were always so cheerful and happy during that time. When they were done decorating, Polaroid's would be taken and hung above the register for others to see. Everyone loved it!

Did anyone ever eat those ginger bread houses? Most of them probably got thrown away or stuffed into a closet somewhere only to be found a year later, petrified and stale. The important thing is that everyone had fun. The kids and parents spent time together without the TV on or continuous video games and YouTube videos playing. The bakery could be a happening place during the holidays.

Latex Gloves

The Deli was also very busy during holiday season for catering parties and company events for up to 500 or 1,000 people. There were many weddings during the holidays, although getting married in one of the coldest seasons doesn't always make a lot of sense. However, with family coming to town it could also make for the perfect time to get married. Honeymooning in the Caribbean during this time, does make sense however. The Swedish meatballs, the meat and cheese trays, stuffed mushrooms, deviled eggs; all got pumped out of the deli and everyone worked overtime and was tired, over-worked, and under-paid! It was a very stressful time of year and one that every deli worker couldn't wait to be over.

The irony was that even though it was the busiest time of year, it was also flu and cold season. It never failed that someone called in sick and then everybody else had to work even harder and longer hours to get everything done on time. When they came back, they got shunned as if they were actually out on a cruise or something, instead of in bed with a 102 degree fever. It's a strange phenomenon; it's best to stay home and keep your germs away from everyone else. However, everyone would rather you came in to work and suffer along with them but then everyone in the department runs the risk of getting sick and that person who was sniffling through their shift gets blamed and never hears the end of it. It's a catch twenty-two.

Observing anyone in the food handling business who is coughing all over the food or wiping their nose seems to turn a lot of people off. That is one of the reasons all bakery workers and deli workers wear latex gloves. Some people keep one pair on all day long and just wash their hands with the gloves on, while some replace their gloves for new ones throughout the day depending on what they are dealing with. For instance, it's very hard to write with the gloves on, so if someone calls in an order and it has to be written down, it's best to remove the gloves, write down the order and put on a new pair. It can be a hassle, but one gets used to it after a while.

The bakery and the deli go through boxes and boxes of latex gloves every month. They come in different sizes; small, medium, and large but it never fails that the medium size always runs out first so the workers have to either pinch their medium-sized hands into small gloves or slop around in oversized gloves.

One year, the deli hired some extra Christmas help on a temporary basis. One of the temps was a very large man named Frank. He was perfect for helping out during the busy holiday season because he was jolly, and round, and had very red cheeks. He was a kind of happy-go-lucky guy who reminded one of Santa Claus. He was in his late 30's and was recently laid off from his other job. He took the temp job because he had a wife and two kids to feed, not to mention buy Christmas gifts for. He would take on whatever job he could get during the holidays and he was very happy to be working at the market to make some money.

During the slow times, Frank would go on unemployment and collect food stamps, but he was healthy and able to work whenever work came his way. He was no social parasite and he always put his best foot forward, even if it was only for $8.50 per hour.

Frank couldn't find any large-sized latex gloves, or any medium-sized gloves. The small size was just out of the question. He asked in the meat department, if they had any large sized gloves around but they didn't. He walked over to the bakery to see if they had any. Nope. They were out of both medium and large! No luck.

Cindy was just coming to work and saw that Frank was somewhat upset. He looked frustrated, his cheeks a bit more red than usual. He didn't want to complain but he told Cindy he couldn't find any gloves to fit his large hands and he thought about going over to the cleaning aisle and purchasing a box of large yellow rubber gloves so that he could finish his shift. Cindy put on her thinking cap, again trying to be the problem-solver and the helper. She remembered when she filled the first aid kits and thought that she stocked them with latex gloves, possibly the larger sized ones. She was fairly certain she had.

Cindy ran over to the closest first aid kit in the store and opened it up. Lo and behold, a pair of large latex gloves! Cindy smiled and handed them to Frank who smiled back and thanked her. He would have to make that one pair last the rest of his shift, but his hands would be protected at least. One day at a time. Cindy was proud of herself for thinking on her feet and for having the foresight to re-stock the first aid kits. Frank was so grateful to Cindy and he gave her a big hug.

Life is very unpredictable. It can be so sad at times and so incredibly happy at others. If we all had a crystal ball that worked, we could map it all out for ourselves, but part of the excitement is never knowing what will happen next. At the market, that was always true. Nobody knew what a day would bring or how many cans of soup would be sold. No one could predict how many injuries would occur or how many people would meet and fall in love in aisle number four. Hearts were broken in the market too. People were fired, hired, and disciplined there. It was like a small city. Anything could happen.

The stories at the market were never-ending. When you have a multitude of people under one roof; employers, employees, customers, etc., both the expected and the unexpected happen. It's time to put this baby to bed until another day, another experience, another moment in life outside of the market.

ABOUT THE AUTHOR

Wendy Allen is from Bellingham, Washington and this is the debut of her first novel, Life at the Market.

The story takes place in a local supermarket and looks behind the scenes at the lives of store employees and customers. It's funny, surprising, and very relatable.

One of her inspirations to write was Anthony Bourdaine's book, Kitchen Confidential. His style really resonated with her and she loved reading about all of his brilliant adventures. The idea to write her own stories became a reality while she was healing from an accident.

Years ago, Wendy was in an electric scooter accident and fell onto a gravel road, scraping up her knee pretty badly. She could hardly walk when the wound became infected and she had to recover with antibiotics. It was during this down time that she began to lose her mind. She read about a jogger who had broken his leg and was also going crazy from just sitting around, so he decided to write a book. Wendy was inspired by his experience and decided to do the same thing to save herself from the boredom.

Please enjoy her "savior" book!

Proof

Made in the USA
Columbia, SC
27 June 2018